"Maybe we could call a truce,"

Val suggested.

"Won't work," Slade said succinctly.

"Why on earth not?"

"Well, the way I see it, you and I are destined to butt heads."

"Because that's the way you want it," Val accused.

Slade grinned. "No. Because you're a woman and I'm a man. Simple as that. It's human nature."

"Sweetheart, if that were human nature, the population would dwindle down to nothing."

Slade gazed directly into her eyes. "Now, you see, *sweetheart,* that's where God steps in. He set it up so all that commotion would be counterbalanced by making up."

Val smiled at him. "Seems to me like you've just given me something to look forward to, cowboy. Let me know anytime you're ready to start making up."

***

Don't miss Sherryl Woods's MIRA Books debut with AFTER TEX, a novel about home, happiness and hardheaded men! Look for AFTER TEX in bookstores mid-September 1999.

Dear Reader,

This September, you may find yourself caught up in the hustle and bustle of a new school year. But as a sensational stress buster, we have an enticing fall lineup for you to pamper yourself with. Each month, we offer six brand-new romances about people just like you—trying to find the perfect balance between life, career, family and love.

For starters, check out *Their Other Mother* by Janis Reams Hudson—a feisty THAT SPECIAL WOMAN! butts head with a gorgeous, ornery father of three. This also marks the debut of this author's engaging new miniseries, WILDERS OF WYATT COUNTY.

Sherryl Woods continues her popular series AND BABY MAKES THREE: THE NEXT GENERATION with an entertaining story about a rodeo champ who becomes victim to his matchmaking daughter in *Suddenly, Annie's Father*. And for those of you who treasure stories about best-friends-turned-lovers, don't miss *That First Special Kiss* by Gina Wilkins, book two in her FAMILY FOUND: SONS AND DAUGHTERS series.

In *Celebrate the Child* by Amy Frazier, a military man becomes an integral part of his precious little girl's life—as well as that of her sweet-natured adopted mom. And when a secret agent takes on the role of daddy, he discovers the family of his dreams in Jane Toombs's *Designated Daddy*. Finally, watch for *A Cowboy's Code* by talented newcomer Alaina Starr, who spins a compelling love story set in the hard-driving West.

I hope you enjoy these six emotional romances created *by* women like you, *for* women like you!

Sincerely,

Karen Taylor Richman
Senior Editor

Please address questions and book requests to:
Silhouette Reader Service
U.S.: 3010 Walden Ave., P.O. Box 1325, Buffalo, NY 14269
Canadian: P.O. Box 609, Fort Erie, Ont. L2A 5X3

SHERRYL WOODS

SUDDENLY, ANNIE'S FATHER

Silhouette®

SPECIAL EDITION®

Published by Silhouette Books
America's Publisher of Contemporary Romance

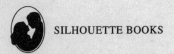

SILHOUETTE BOOKS

ISBN 0-373-24268-9

SUDDENLY, ANNIE'S FATHER

Visit us at www.romance.net

Printed in U.S.A.

SHERRYL WOODS

Whether she's living in California, Florida or Virginia, Sherryl Woods always makes her home by the sea. A walk on the beach, the sound of waves, the smell of the salt air, all provide inspiration for this writer of more than sixty romance and mystery novels. Sherryl hopes you're enjoying this latest entry in the AND BABY MAKES THREE series for Silhouette Special Edition. You can write to Sherryl, or—from April through December—stop by and meet her at her bookstore, Potomac Sunrise, 308 Washington Avenue, Colonial Beach, VA 22443.

Harlan Patrick and Laurie Adams
announce the marriage of their friends
Val Harding and Slade Sutton
and welcome them
and their daughter, Annie,
to the White Pines Family

Chapter One

Slade Sutton knew a whole lot about horses, but he didn't know a blasted thing about females. The only woman with whom he'd ever risked his heart had damn near killed him in a car crash, then divorced him when he could not longer win rodeo championships. Worse, she'd left him with a daughter who was a total mystery to him.

Annie was ten-going-on-thirty, wise beyond her years, clever as the dickens and the prettiest little girl he'd ever seen, even if he was a mite biased on the subject. While he'd been on the circuit, they'd been apart more than they'd been together, which had left both of them as wary as if they'd been strangers.

Ever since the accident and Suzanne's desertion, Annie had been living with his parents, but he knew the time was fast approaching when he would no longer be able to shirk his responsibilities. He'd begun dreading every phone call, knowing that most spelled trouble. Annie had a knack for it, and his parents' level of tolerance was slipping. He could hear it in their tired voices. He'd been making excuses for weeks now for not going home for a visit. He'd half feared they'd sneak Annie into his truck on his way out of town. Every night he prayed she'd stay out of mischief just a little longer, just until he could get his bearings in this new job.

Of course, he'd been working for Harlan and Cody Adams for nearly a year now at White Pines, caring for their horses, setting up a breeding program, breaking the yearlings. He could hardly claim he was still getting settled, but he dreaded the day when his parents called him on it.

He studied the picture of Annie that he kept on his bedside table and shook his head in wonder. How had he had any part in producing a child so beautiful, so delicately feminine? He lived in a rough-and-tumble world. She looked like a fairy-tale princess, a little angel.

Judging from the reports he'd been receiving, however, looks could be deceiving. Annie was as spirited as any bronco he'd ever ridden. She charged at life full throttle and, like him, she didn't know the meaning of fear.

The phone on the bunkhouse wall rang, cutting into his wandering thoughts. Hardy Jones grabbed for it. Hardy had more women chasing after him than a Hollywood movie star. It had become a joke around the ranch. No one saw much use to Hardy's pretense of living in the bunkhouse, when he never spent a night in his bed there. And no one besides Hardy ever jumped for the phone.

"Hey, Slade, it's for you," the cowboy called out, looking disappointed.

Trepidation stirred in Slade's gut as he crossed the room. It had to be trouble. Annie had been too much on his mind today. That was a surefire sign that something was going on over in Wilder's Glen, Texas.

Sure enough, it was his father, sounding grim.

"Dadgumit, Slade, you're going to have to come and get your daughter," Harold Sutton decreed without wasting much time on idle chitchat.

Much as he wanted to ignore it, even Slade could hear the desperation in his father's voice. He sighed. "What's Annie done now?"

"Aside from falling out of a tree and breaking her wrist, climbing on the roof and darn near bringing down the chimney, I suppose you could say she's having a right peaceful summer," his father said. "But she's a handful, Son, and your mama and I just can't cope with her anymore. We've been talking it over for a while now. We're too dadgum old for this. We don't have the kind of energy it takes to keep up with her."

Slade's father was an ex-marine and had his own garage. He put in ten hours a day there and played golf every chance he got. His mother gardened, canned vegetables, made quilts and belonged to every single organization in Wilder's Glen. Slade wasn't buying the idea that they couldn't keep up with a ten-year-old. Annie had just stretched their patience, that was all. It had to be.

"Look, whatever she's done, I'm sure she didn't mean to. I'll talk to her, get her to settle down a little."

"This isn't just about settling her down," his father countered. "She needs you."

The last thing Slade wanted was to be needed by anyone, especially a ten-year-old girl. Between the aches and pains that reminded him every second of the accident that had cost him his career and very nearly his life, and the anger at the woman responsible, it was all he could do to get through the day on his own. He was grateful every single minute of it, though, that his parents had been willing to take Annie in when he hadn't been up to it. She'd been better off with them than she would have been with him. He'd been too bitter, too filled with resentment toward her mama to be any kind of example for an impressionable kid.

"You know I'm grateful," he began.

"We don't want your thanks," his father said, cutting him off. "We love Annie and we love you. We know the jam you were in after the accident. We understood you needed some time to get back on your feet."

"But—"

"Let me finish now. Your mama and I aren't up to raising Annie the way the girl ought to be raised. We had a houseful of boys. Girls just aren't the same, even though Annie seems bent on being the toughest little tomboy in the whole town. Besides that, times have changed since you and your brothers were kids. The world's a different place.''

''Not in Wilder's Glen,'' Slade protested. ''It's perfect for Annie. It's a small town. She'll be as safe there as she could be anywhere.''

''Her safety's not the only issue. Even if it were, she'll be just as safe in Los Piños. No, indeed, there's a more important issue, and you know it. She misses you. She belongs with you. We were glad enough to fill in for a while, but it's time for you to take over now and that's that. Otherwise the child will be scarred for life, thinking that her own daddy didn't want her any more than her mama did.''

''But—''

''No buts, and you can forget coming after her. We'll bring her to you this weekend,'' Harold announced decisively, as if he no longer trusted Slade to show up for her.

Slade sighed heavily. The sorry truth was he wouldn't have, not even with a deadline staring him in the face. He would have called at the last minute with some excuse or another, and counted on his parents to hang in with Annie a little longer.

Hearing a date and time for assuming responsibility for his daughter all but made Slade's skin crawl. Much as he loved Annie, he wasn't cut out to be a parent to her. His experience with her mother was pretty much evidence of his lack of understanding of the female mind. He was also flat-out terrified that the resentment he felt toward Suzanne would carry over to their daughter in some way he wouldn't be able to control. No kid deserved that.

Annie was the spitting image of his ex-wife in every way, from her gloriously thick hair to her green-as-emerald eyes, from the dusting of freckles on her nose to her stubborn chin. Apparently she had her mama's wicked ways about her, too. She'd caused more trouble in the last year than any child he'd ever known. She'd topped his own imaginative forms of rebellion by a mile and she hadn't even hit puberty yet. What on earth would her teenage years hold? To be fair, he couldn't blame his parents for not wanting to find out.

"Are you sure?" he asked, his own voice desperate now. "I don't think it's such a good idea for her to come here. She's comfortable there with you. She's starting to think of that as home. She spent the school year there. She's made friends. Uprooting her all over again won't be good for her. Besides that, the Adamses don't even know I have a daughter. I'm living in a bunkhouse. Some days I don't get to bed till midnight and I'm back up again at dawn."

He'd ticked off a half-dozen excuses before he was done, most of them flat-out lies. He knew that a staunch family man like Harlan Adams would never object to Slade bringing his daughter to the ranch. If anything, he'd be furious Slade hadn't brought her to be with him before now.

As for the living arrangements, Harlan Adams would make adjustments for that, too. It had been Slade's choice to live in the bunkhouse, rather than one of the other homes dotted across Adams land. He'd wanted to stay close to the horses that were his responsibility. Horses were something he understood.

He tried one last panicked ploy. "I could get you some help," he offered. "Maybe a housekeeper."

"This isn't about cooking and cleaning," his father scoffed. "It's about a little girl needing her daddy. We're coming Sunday and that's that."

There was a finality to his tone with which Slade was all too familiar. Just to emphasize his point, Harold hung up before Slade could think of a single argument to convince him to keep Annie with them.

"Looks like it's time to face the music, bud," he muttered under his breath. Way past time, some would say.

Resigned to his fate, first thing in the morning he arranged to sit down with Cody Adams to discuss his housing situation.

"If there's no place available, I can call my folks back and tell them to give me more time to work it out," he told Cody, praying for a reprieve.

"Absolutely not," Cody said at once, then grinned at Slade's heavy sigh. "Uh-oh, were you counting on me to bail you out of this?"

"I suppose I was," Slade admitted. "Annie and I haven't spent a lot of time together. I'm not sure how good I'll be at this parent thing."

"Then you're lucky you're here. Anytime you're at a loss, just ask one of us for help." The rancher's expression turned sly. "I know one woman who'd be glad to step in and do a little mothering if Annie needs it."

An image of Val Harding came to mind without Cody even having to mention her name. A petite whirlwind with a nonstop mouth, she had set her

sights on Slade during a visit to the ranch a few
months back. She hadn't let up since. Thankfully, she
was in Nashville right now with her boss, country
music superstar Laurie Jensen, who was married to
Cody's son.

"Thanks all the same," Slade said curtly. "Last I
heard Val was out of town."

Cody's grin spread. "Got back last night. The way
I hear it from Harlan Patrick, Laurie's going to take
a break for a while. She'll be working on the songs
for her next album. Val should have plenty of time
on her hands."

"I just hope she finds a way to spend it besides
pestering me," Slade muttered.

"What was that?"

"Nothing."

Thankfully, Cody let the subject drop. He held out
a key. "Check out that house down by the creek. It's
been vacant since Joe and his wife left. It's probably
a little dusty, but it should be fine for the two of you
once it's aired out and had a good cleaning. If it needs
anything—dishes, extra blankets, whatever—let me
know. I'll get somebody to handle the horses today.
You get the place ready. Call up to the main house.
One of Maritza's helpers can come down to give you
a hand."

"No need," Slade said. "I'll take care of whatever
needs to be done. Thanks, Cody. I owe you."

Cody regarded him speculatively. "Family counts
for a lot around here. We'll welcome Annie as if she
were one of us. You can rest easy on that score."

Slade knew he meant it, too. The Adamses were

good people. Maybe they would be able to make up for whatever he lacked.

He took the key Cody offered and headed toward the small house made of rough-hewn wood. It wasn't fancy, but there was a certain charm to it, he supposed. Pots of bright red geraniums bloomed on the porch and a big old cottonwood tree shaded the yard. The creek flowed past just beyond.

The house had been closed up since the last tenant had left, a married hand who'd retired and moved to Arizona. A cursory glance around the small rooms told Slade it had everything he and Annie could need, including a small TV that had been hooked up to cable. The kitchen was well stocked with dishes and pots and pans. Fortunately, the refrigerator had a good-size freezer, big enough to accommodate all the prepared meals he and Annie were likely to consume. His cooking skills ran to cold cereal and boiled eggs.

The closets revealed a supply of linens for the beds, a small one in what would be Annie's room, and a big brass bed with a feather mattress in what was clearly the master bedroom. Staring at that mattress was disconcerting. All sorts of wicked images came to mind, images of being tangled up with a woman again. One particular woman, he conceded with some dismay. He could all but feel her breath on his chest and sense the weight of her head tucked under his chin. It had been a long time since he'd allowed himself to indulge in the fantasy, much less the reality.

"Quite a bed, isn't it?" an all-too-familiar voice inquired with a seductive purr.

Slade scowled at the intrusion by the pesky woman

whose image had just flitted through his mind. "You ever heard of knocking?" he asked.

Val didn't flinch at his impatient tone. "I wasn't sure anyone was in here. Nobody's been living here and the front door was standing open. I was afraid someone had broken in."

Slade regarded her incredulously. "So you decided to do what—wander in and talk them to death? Didn't it occur to you that if a robber was in here, you could get hurt?"

She grinned, looking smug. "Worried about me, cowboy? That's progress."

She slipped past him into the room, leaving a cloud of perfume in her wake. Slade tried not to let the scent stir him the way it usually did. Sometimes he thought he smelled that soft, flowery aroma in the middle of the night. Those were the nights he tossed and turned till dawn and cursed the day Val had come to live at White Pines and taken an interest in him.

"Nice view," she observed, gazing out at the creek. "What are you doing here, by the way?"

"Moving in," he said, backing out of the room before his body could get any ideas about tossing her onto that feather mattress to see if it—and she—were as soft as he imagined.

She turned slowly. "Alone?"

"No."

Something that might have been disappointment flared briefly in her eyes. "I see."

Guilt over that look had him admitting the truth. "My daughter's coming to stay with me." He tested the words aloud and found they didn't cause quite so much panic since his talk with Cody. Knowing he'd have backup had eased his mind. Maybe Annie could survive having a father as inept as him, after all.

Val's expression brightened with curiosity. She seized on the tidbit as if he'd tossed her the hottest piece of gossip since the world had discovered that singer Laurie Jensen had a secret baby by the man who was now her husband.

"You have a daughter?" she asked. "How old? What's she like? Where's she been all this time? What about her mother?"

Slade grinned despite himself. "You care to try those one at a time?"

"Oh, just tell me everything and save us both the aggravation," she retorted. "I wouldn't have to pester you so if you'd open up in the first place."

"Is that so? And here I thought you enjoyed pestering me."

"Getting you to talk is a challenge," she admitted. "And you know how we women react to a challenge."

He regarded her intently. "So, if I just blab away, you'll go away eventually?"

She grinned. "Maybe. Try it and see."

"Sorry. I'm too busy right now. Maybe another time."

The dismissal didn't even faze her. "Busy doing what? Looked to me like you were daydreaming when I came in."

"Which is why it's all the more important for me to get started with the work around here now," he said, and headed for the kitchen again. He'd seen

cleaning supplies in there on his first stop. He
snatched up a broom, a vacuum, dust cloths and fur-
niture polish. He figured he could give the place a
decent once-over in an hour and be back on the job
before noon.

Val reached for the broom. "Give me that. I'll
help."

Slade held tight. "There's no need. You'll ruin
your clothes."

The woman always dressed as if she were about to
meet with the press or go out for cocktails. He
doubted she owned a pair of jeans or sneakers, much
less boots. In fact, today was one of the rare occasions
when she wasn't wearing those ridiculous high heels
she paraded around in. He had to admit those shoes
did a lot for her legs. It was almost a disappointment
when she traded them for flats, as she had today.

In flats, she barely came up to his chin, reminding
him of just how fragile and utterly feminine a creature
she was. It brought out the protective instincts in him,
despite the fact that there wasn't a doubt in his mind
that Val Harding could look out for herself. Heaven
knew, she protected Laurie with a ferocity that was
daunting. No one got anywhere close to the singer
without Val's approval. Slade secretly admired that
kind of loyalty. Too bad Suzanne hadn't possessed
even a quarter as much. They might have stayed married.

"Oh, for heaven's sakes, give me the broom," Val
said. "A little dust never hurt anything. You'll get
finished that much sooner if you let me help. Other-

wise, I'll just trail around after you asking more questions you don't want to answer.''

She had a point about that. It wasn't likely she'd respond to his dismissal and just go away. Reluctantly, Slade relinquished the broom and watched as she went to work with a vengeance on the wide-plank oak floors in the living room. She attacked the job with the same cheerfulness and efficiency with which she ran Laurie's professional life.

When she glanced up and caught Slade staring at her, she grinned. "Get to work. I said I'd help, not do the whole job."

"Yes, ma'am," he said at once, and turned on the vacuum. As he ran it over the carpet in the bedrooms, he could hear her singing with wildly off-key enthusiasm. He wondered if Laurie had ever heard one of her country music hits murdered quite the way Val was doing it.

With her help, he had the house tidied up in no time. Fresh air was drifting through the rooms and filling them with the sweet scent of recently cut grass and a hint of Janet's roses from the gardens at the main house.

An odd sensation came over him as he stood in the living room and gazed about, listening to Val stirring around in the kitchen. The place felt like home, like some place a man could put down roots. For a man who'd spent most of his adult life on the road, it was a terrifying sensation.

Slade Sutton was the most exasperating, frustrating man on the face of the earth. Val watched him take off without so much as a thank-you. He looked as if he were being chased by demons as he fled the house. The limp from his accident was more exaggerated as he tried to move quickly. She knew his expression, if she'd been able to see his face, would be filled with annoyance over his ungainly gait and, most of all, over her.

Of course, he had that look a lot when he was trying to get away from her, she admitted with a sigh. It had been months since she'd first met him, and she could honestly say that she didn't know him one bit better now than she had when she'd paid her first visit to White Pines.

No, that wasn't quite true. Today she'd learned he had a daughter. Amazing. How could anyone keep a secret like that, especially around the Adamses, who made her look like an amateur when it came to nosing into other people's lives? Laurie had tried to keep Harlan Patrick's baby a secret from him and that had lasted less than six months. Of course, the tabloids had had a hand in leaking that news and sending Harlan Patrick chasing after Laurie.

A lot of women would have given up if they'd had the same reception from Slade that Val had had. Why go through the torment of rejection after rejection? Why poke and prod and get nothing but a shrug or a grunted acknowledgment for her persistence? She'd asked herself that a hundred times while she'd been in Nashville this last time. She'd hoped that a little distance from the ranch would give her some perspective, maybe dull the attraction she felt for him. After all, Slade Sutton wasn't the last man on earth.

But he was the only one in years who'd intrigued her, the only one who hadn't been using her to get closer to Laurie. In fact, he was the only man she knew who barely spared a glance for the gorgeous superstar. Val had caught him looking at her, though, sneaking glances when he thought she wasn't aware of him. Maybe that hint of interest, reluctant as it was, was what kept her going.

Or maybe it had something to do with how incredibly male he was. Handsome as sin, a little rough around the edges, he had eyes a woman could drown in. She'd discovered that when he finally took off his sunglasses long enough to allow anyone to catch a glimpse of them. A dimple flirted at the corner of his mouth on the rare occasions when he smiled. His jaw looked as if it had been carved from granite. In fact, he was all hard angles and solid muscle, the kind of man whose strength wasn't obtained in a gym, but just from living.

Bottom line? He made her mouth water. She sometimes thought that if he didn't kiss her soon, she was going to have to take matters into her own hands.

Then again, she preferred to think she wasn't quite so shallow. That it wasn't all about lust and sex. Maybe she just liked a good mystery.

Slade was certainly that. He'd told the Adamses no more than he had to to get hired. He'd told her even less. There'd been times in the last six months when she'd found that so thoroughly frustrating she'd been tempted to hire a private investigator to fill in the gaps, but that would have spoiled the game. She wanted to unearth his secrets all on her own. It was turning out to be a time-consuming task. At the rate of one revelation every few months, she'd be at it for a lifetime.

It was a good thing her daddy had taught her about grit. Nobody on the face of the earth was more determined or more persistent than she was. She'd used those lessons to get the job she wanted in Nashville, pestering Laurie's agent until he'd made the introduction just to get her out of his office. Now she was personal assistant to the hottest country music star in the country. Those same lessons made her the best at what she did.

Now they were going to help her get Slade Sutton, too.

She watched him hightail it back toward the barn and his precious horses. She grinned, understanding fully for the first time that she made him nervous. He was every bit as skittish as one of those new colts he found to be such a challenge. That was good. It was a vast improvement over indifference.

Yes, indeed, he could run, but he couldn't hide, she concluded with satisfaction. Laurie was home for a much-deserved breather, and Val had a whole lot of time on her hands. Slade didn't stand a chance.

Chapter Two

Sunday morning dawned with a sudden storm that rivaled the turmoil churning in Slade's gut. Lightning and thunder split the air. From inside the house, he could see the creek rising rapidly, though it was not yet in danger of overflowing its banks as it had on a few terrifying occasions in past summers. Just a few years ago, he'd been told, it had flooded out this house, destroying most of the previous tenants' belongings and washing away a lifetime of memories. In the tenacious manner of the Adamses and everyone around them, they had cleaned it up without complaint and started over.

He shuddered at another crack of thunder, though his unease had more to do with the next few hours than with the storm. Annie would be here all too soon.

He had no idea how she felt about him these days. On his few visits to Wilder's Glen, she had been withdrawn, clearly blaming him for the changes in her life.

As for him, he was nowhere near ready to deal with the changes her arrival would bring to his life. Oh, he'd made a few preparations. He'd moved his things over to their house. He'd gone into town and picked up enough frozen dinners to last for a month. The freezer was so crowded with them, there wasn't even room for ice cubes.

He'd even gone into a toy store and impulsively bought a huge stuffed bear to sit in the middle of Annie's bed. When she was little, he'd bought her a stuffed toy or a doll every time he'd come home. She's always loved them then. Her eyes had lit up with unabashed joy and she'd crawled into his lap, hugging the latest toy tightly in her arms. Her smile had wiped away the guilt he'd always felt at leaving her behind. Maybe it would work one more time.

He trudged over to the barn through the pouring rain, finished up his chores, regretting the fact that they didn't take longer. When he was through, he went back to the house to shower and wait. That gave him way too much time to think, to remember the way his life had been not so long ago.

He'd been a celebrity of sorts, a champion, whose whole identity had been wrapped up in winning rodeos. He'd had plenty of money in the bank. He'd had a beautiful, headstrong wife who could turn him on with a glance, and a daughter who awed and amazed him. Life was exciting, a never-ending round of facing the unexpected. There'd been media attention and applause and physical challenges.

What did he have now? A decent-paying job working at one of the best ranches in Texas. It was steady employment, no surprises. That's what he'd told himself he wanted after Suzanne had walked out. Routine and boredom had seemed attractive after the turbulence of their last few weeks together. No emotional entanglements, not even with his own kid. He sighed heavily as he considered the selfishness of that.

He'd pay for it now, no doubt about it. Annie was no longer the joyous, carefree sprite she'd been a year ago. Suzanne was to blame for some of that, but he had to shoulder the rest. It was up to him to make up for the fact that Annie's mother had walked out on both of them. If he'd been neglectful in the months since, Suzanne had been cruel. He knew for a fact she hadn't written or called in all that time.

Rainwater dripped from the roof as he watched and waited. The summer storm finally ended almost as quickly as it had begun, leaving the air steamy and the dirt driveway a sea of mud. Dirt splattered every which way when his father's car finally came barreling in just after one o'clock. Slade grinned at the sight. His father was driving the way he always did, as if he were ten minutes late for a military dress parade. The marine in him had never fully died.

Slade stepped off the porch and went to greet them, wrapping his mother in a bear hug that had her laughing. Only when he'd released her did he notice the exhaustion in her eyes, the tired lines around her mouth. Surely she hadn't looked that old the last time he'd seen her. Knowing the toll Annie had taken on her was just one more thing for him to feel guilty about.

He studied his father intently as he shook his hand. He didn't see any noticeable changes in Harold Sutton's appearance. His close-cropped hair had been gray for years, so Slade couldn't blame that on Annie. His grip was as strong as ever, his manner as brusque and hearty. He didn't look like the kind of man who'd let a child get the better of him. Slade had to wonder if that hadn't just been an excuse to force him to take Annie back into his life.

"Good to see you, Son."

"You, too, Dad."

"Annie, girl, get on out here and say hello to your daddy," Harold Sutton commanded in a booming voice left from his days as a marine drill sergeant. None of his sons had ever dared to ignore one of his orders. Punishments for disobedience had been doled out swiftly. For a minute, though, Slade thought that Annie might. She stared out at them from the back seat, her expression mulish.

Eventually, though, she slipped out of the car with obvious reluctance and stood there awkwardly, refusing to come closer. It was all Slade could do not to gape when he saw her.

How the devil had his daughter gone from being a little angel in frilly dresses to *this?* he wondered, staring at the ripped jeans, baggy T-shirt and filthy sneakers Annie was wearing. He'd been prepared for the cast on her arm, but not for the fact that it appeared she'd been rolling in mud wearing it.

And what the dickens had happened to her curls? The last time he'd seen her, she'd had pretty, chestnut-colored hair, braided neatly and tied with bows. Now it looked as if someone had taken a pair of dull scissors and whacked it off about two inches from her scalp.

Annie regarded him with a sullen expression, while he tried to figure out what to say to her.

"You look real good," he managed finally.

Annie didn't even waste her breath replying to the blatant lie. She just continued to stare at him with a defiant tilt to her chin and a heartbreaking mix of hurt and anger in her eyes. He might have responded to that, if his mother hadn't latched onto his arm and pulled him aside.

"I'll explain to you about that later," she muttered under her breath, her gaze pointedly focused on Annie's hairstyle. "Please don't say anything about her hair. She's very self-conscious about it."

"She darned well ought to be," Slade retorted. "What were you thinking?"

"It wasn't me," she snapped. "When she found out we were bringing her over here, she did it herself."

He shot a bewildered glance toward his daughter. "But why?"

"I have no idea. She's a mystery, Slade. Keeps everything bottled up inside. It comes out in these daredevil acts of hers. I never know what kind of trouble she's going to get herself into. She's a smart girl, but you saw her report cards. She got through the school year by the skin of her teeth. I'm pretty sure her principal will throw a party when she hears Annie's transferring to another school district.''

She gestured toward the three suitcases his father had lined up on the porch. "That's everything she has. Your dad and I will be going now," she said, as if she couldn't wait to get away, to get some peace and quiet back into her life.

Slade stared at her in shock. "You can't leave," he protested. The nastiest bull on the circuit had never set off such panic deep inside him.

"It's a long way back home. Tomorrow's a workday for your daddy. Besides, you two need time to settle in.''

"But you've driven all this way. I thought we'd go into town for a nice dinner or something," he said, trying to delay the inevitable moment when he and his daughter would be left on their own.

His mother gave him a sympathetic pat. "Everything's going to work out just fine, Son. She's your own flesh and blood, after all. All the girl needs is a little love and attention from her daddy. You remember how she used to worship the ground you walked on. She was a daddy's girl, no doubt about it. She never mentions her mama, but I catch her staring at the pictures we have of you on the mantel.''

Love and attention, Slade thought, staring at Annie uneasily after his parents had driven away. Too bad those were the two things likely to be in very short supply coming from him.

Val stood in the office Harlan Patrick had built for her just off her boss's music room and stared at the scene outside. It was like watching an accident unfold in slow motion, horrifying and tragic. Slade Sutton was regarding his daughter as if she were a rattler he considered capable of striking at any second. His wariness was downright pathetic, but then Slade seemed to be wary of most females.

Watching him with his daughter, she couldn't hear what was being said, but it was all too evident that neither of them had conversational skills worth a hill of beans. The few feet between them might as well have been a mile.

Hug her, Val coached silently. Neither of them budged. Slade's hands were jammed into his pockets. His daughter's were jammed into her own. It was as if they both feared reaching out. Val wondered if Slade even realized that the girl was mimicking his mannerisms.

Abruptly he turned and stalked away. As the girl stared after him, her chin wobbled as if she might cry, but then she, too, turned and stalked off, in the opposite direction. Her suitcases stayed where they'd been left, right on the porch. He hadn't even bothered to take her inside and show her where she'd be living.

"They're a sorry pair, aren't they?" Laurie asked, coming to stand beside her. "I was watching from upstairs. I guess it's true what I heard, that they'd been estranged for months now. I wonder why."

"The why's not important. Somebody needs to see to that poor child," Val said, her indignation rising. "Slade's obviously not going to do it."

"Why don't you go?" Laurie suggested, regarding her with amusement. "You know you want to.

You've been itching to find out more about Slade's daughter ever since you discovered he had one.''

Val shook her head and reluctantly turned away from the window. ''I don't want to meddle.''

Laurie grinned. ''That'll be a first. When it comes to meddling, you could rival Grandpa Harlan. If I didn't know better, I'd swear you were an Adams. My relationship with Harlan Patrick wasn't any of your business, either, but that didn't keep you from teaming up with him.''

''That was different. You two belonged together. You were just too stubborn to admit it. You needed a little push.''

''Maybe that's all those two need.''

''Forget it. You know how Slade is. He'll be furious if I go sticking my nose into his business,'' she said, fighting the temptation to meddle anyway. Another glance at that downcast child and she'd let her heart overrule her common sense.

''Since when did his moods bother you?'' Laurie asked. ''Besides, I thought you took great satisfaction in provoking him.''

Laurie was right about that. Val did like getting Slade Sutton all stirred up. Every now and again the fire she managed to spark in his eyes struck her as very promising. So far, he'd carefully avoided indulging in anything remotely close to a passionate response. In fact, he made it a point to steer clear of her whenever he could. Yesterday had been one of those rare occasions when running hadn't been an option.

One day, though, she was going to catch him alone

when he didn't have chores to tend to. She would seize the chance to deliberately push him over the edge. Then she'd finally discover if all this chemistry she'd been feeling for the past few months was one-sided or not.

Now was not the time, however, and Annie was not the best subject to use to provoke a response from him. There were too many complicated emotions at work here that Val didn't understand.

After she thought for a minute about the scene she'd just witnessed, it occurred to her that for once Slade might be grateful to have her step in. Clearly he was out of his depth, though why that should be eluded her.

She, on the other hand, liked kids. All sorts of maternal feelings washed through her every time she held Laurie's baby. Now that Amy Lynn was beginning to toddle around on unsteady legs, Val enjoyed chasing after her almost as much as she liked setting up interviews and keeping Laurie's life on track. She might not have signed on as a baby-sitter, but it was one of the duties she took on willingly.

"Okay, okay," she agreed finally, giving in to Laurie's urging and her own desire to get involved. "I'm going." She said it as if she were caving in to pressure, just to preserve the illusion of reluctance. The truth was she was eager to meet Slade's daughter, just as Laurie had said.

Outside, she strolled casually in the direction in which she'd seen the child go. Surprisingly, she found her near the stables. Apparently she'd gravitated back toward where she knew her father would be, after all.

Slade was nowhere in sight, but Val assumed he was inside the barn doing those endless chores he found so fascinating.

"Hi," Val said, coming up to the corral railing to stand beside her. "I'm Val."

The girl kept her gaze focused on the horses.

"You must be Annie," Val continued, as if she hadn't been totally ignored. Apparently father and child shared a disdain for polite responses. "I've been hearing a lot about you."

"Not from my dad, I'll bet," Annie responded, giving her a sullen glance.

"Actually, that's not true. Your dad is the one who told me you were coming. Then I heard about you again from my boss, Laurie Jensen."

The mention of Laurie's name was bound to catch the attention of anyone who'd ever listened to country music. Laurie's albums were at the top of the charts. Annie Sutton proved to be no exception. She regarded Val suspiciously.

"Yeah, right. Like you actually know Laurie Jensen."

"Like I said, I work for her." She gestured vaguely toward Harlan Patrick's house, which wasn't visible from where they stood. "She lives about a quarter mile down the road, not too far from your dad's house. Surely he's mentioned that to you."

Annie shrugged. "Me and my dad don't talk too much." She focused her attention on the horses for a while, then asked, "So, how come Laurie Jensen lives here?"

"She's married to Harlan Patrick Adams, who's one of the owners of this ranch."

There was a flash of interest in eyes that had been way too bored for any typically inquisitive ten-year-old. "No way."

"It's true."

Her expression brightened visibly. "And you said Laurie Jensen actually knew my name?"

Val grinned at her astonishment. "She did."

"Awesome."

Relieved to have caught the child's interest, Val decided to capitalize on it. Maybe she could forge a bond with Annie more easily than she'd imagined. "Maybe you could come by sometime and meet her, listen to her working on songs for her next album. If your dad doesn't mind, that is."

Annie's excited expression faded. "Oh, he won't care. He doesn't want me here, anyway."

Even though she'd suspected as much, Val was still shocked by the words, angered by the fact that Slade had let his feelings show so plainly. "I'm sure that's not true."

"Yes, it is. He hates me."

"Why on earth would he hate you? You're his daughter," Val protested, unwilling to believe there could be any truth to the accusation.

"It's because of my mom. She almost got him killed when she drove his car into a ditch, and then she left us," she said matter-of-factly. "I guess I don't blame him for hating me. Everybody says I look just like her. I heard Grandma tell one of her friends that if I'm not careful I'll turn out just like her, too. Nothing but trouble, that's what she said.''

Val was stunned. This was more than she'd ever learned from Slade, and it went a long way toward explaining his attitude toward women. Still, his problems with his ex-wife were no excuse for treating his daughter the way he'd been doing. And her grandmother should have watched her tongue. Val couldn't see that it served any useful purpose to go knocking her former daughter-in-law where Annie could overhear her.

"Your mom's leaving must have hurt you both very much," Val said, treading carefully. "Sometimes grown-ups don't get over something like that very easily."

"Like kids do?" Annie retorted. She sighed heavily, as if resigned to the fact that no adult could ever understand what she was going through.

"Of course not," Val agreed, "but—"

Annie faced her squarely. "Look, you don't have to be nice to me. I'm just a kid and I'm used to being on my own. My grandma and grandpa pretty much left me alone, except when I did something wrong."

"I'll bet you got into trouble a lot then, didn't you?" Val guessed.

Annie stared at her with obvious surprise. "How'd you know that?" She sighed once again. "Never mind. I suppose *he* told you. He probably warned you about me."

Val decided not to tell her it was predictable. Annie probably thought she was the only kid who'd ever used that technique to get the attention of the adults around her. "Nope. Lucky guess," she said instead. She glanced toward the horses. "Do you like horses as much as your dad does?"

Annie shrugged. "I suppose. My grandma and grandpa lived in town, so we didn't have horses."

"But you must have been around them when your dad was on the rodeo circuit."

"Me and my mom didn't go with him all that much after I started school. I guess we did when I was real little, but I don't remember that. My mom said it was my fault he left us behind all the time."

Val hid her dismay. What kind of mother openly blamed her child for the problems that were clearly between her and her husband? And what kind of father allowed it to happen? She wanted to reach out and hug this sad, neglected child, but Annie's defensive posture told her she wouldn't welcome the gesture, much less trust that it was genuine.

"You're going to really love living here," Val told her instead. "There are lots of kids around. The Adamses are wonderful people. They'll throw a party at the drop of a hat. You'll fit in in no time."

Annie looked skeptical. "They probably won't invite my dad and me. He just works here."

"I work here, too, but they always include me."

"You're a grown-up," Annie said, but she couldn't hide the wistful look that crossed her face.

"Maybe so, but I was hoping maybe we could be friends. I haven't been here all that long myself. Maybe we could go into town one day. I could show you around while your dad's working."

Annie regarded her skeptically. "Yeah, well, if

you're doing it so my dad'll notice you, you're wasting your time. He hates girls, because of my mom. My grandma says he'd be a recluse if he could.''

Apparently Grandma had one very loose tongue. "Well, you're here now, so being a recluse is not an option,'' Val said briskly, giving Annie's shoulder a reassuring squeeze. "He may not know it yet, but having you here is going to be very good for him. I can tell that already.''

Despite Annie's conviction about how little her father thought of her, she gave Val a hopeful look that almost broke her heart.

"Do you think so?'' she asked.

"I know so,'' Val assured her. If she had to knock Slade Sutton upside the head herself, she was going to see to it.

Chapter Three

Val had a giant-size calendar spread out on the floor in Laurie's music room, while her boss sprawled on the sofa, idly picking out a tune on her guitar.

"This song is terrible," Laurie concluded, eyeing the instrument as if it were at fault. "I haven't been able to write worth a lick since Harlan Patrick and I got married."

"Stop putting so much pressure on yourself," Val advised. She'd been listening to the same complaint for weeks now. If Laurie wasn't careful, she was going to talk herself straight into a writer's block, even though on her worst days she was better than half the songwriters out there. "Take time out to count your blessings. You have a handsome, sexy husband who adores you. You have a gorgeous daughter who is absolutely brilliant for someone barely a year old."

Laurie managed a ghost of a smile at the reminders. "Okay, yes, I am very lucky."

"Concentrate on that for a few days. After all, you only need two more songs for the new album," she reminded her boss. "The studio time's not booked for two more months."

The faint smile faded at once. "Why two months?" Laurie grumbled, picking out the notes of her last hit on the guitar. "I should be in Nashville now. If I don't get back to work soon, my fans will forget all about me."

Val rolled her eyes heavenward. Laurie had been a wreck ever since she had agreed to take a break from her usual hectic recording and concert pace. She blamed her agent, Val and Harlan Patrick for talking her into it. Most of all, she blamed herself for caving in. The forced idleness was making her crazy, especially since her husband was as busy as ever running the ranch and couldn't devote himself full-time to keeping her occupied.

"No one is going to forget about you," Val soothed. "Nick and I have that covered. There will be plenty of items in the media. I've booked you on at least one of the entertainment shows every single month until the album's due to be released. There are fresh angles for every story. Besides, I thought you had enough media coverage to last a lifetime when they were chasing after the story of your secret baby."

Laurie didn't look pacified. "What if Harlan Patrick was right?"

"About what?"

"What if I refused to marry him for so long because I knew once I was completely happy I wouldn't be able to write another song?"

"Oh, for heaven's sakes, that is the most ridiculous thing I've ever heard. You don't have to be wallowing in heartbreak to know what it's like. Draw on old memories. For that matter, write something upbeat for a change." She gave Laurie a wicked smile. "Write about having babies."

Laurie's scowl deepened. "Now you sound exactly like Harlan Patrick. He wants me barefoot and pregnant."

"Maybe that's because he missed seeing you pregnant with Amy Lynn. Maybe he just wants to be in on the next pregnancy from start to finish. Maybe it's not some evil scheme to see you trapped down here on the ranch."

Laurie sighed. "I suppose."

"You know what I think?"

"What?"

"I think you're already pregnant."

Laurie's idle strumming screeched into something wildly discordant. "Oh, God. Bite your tongue."

"Stop it," Val chided. "This is exactly the mood you were in when you were carrying Amy Lynn. To be honest, you were unbearable. Of course, then it was understandable. You had to hide out so Harlan Patrick wouldn't find out about the baby. There's no need to hide out now. You can go on the road. You can do anything you'd do if you weren't pregnant. It wouldn't be a calamity, Laurie. And Harlan Patrick and the rest of the family would be over the moon at the news.''

"I suppose," Laurie conceded, clearly unconvinced. She glanced down at the calendar Val had been working on. "What are you doing?"

"Trying to finalize next spring's concert tour."

Laurie's expression brightened. "Let me see," she said, putting the guitar aside to kneel down beside Val. "Dallas, Tucson, San Antonio, Phoenix, Albuquerque, Denver. Why is everything in the Southwest? Does Nick know something I don't? Am I losing fans in the South?"

"No, you are not losing fans anywhere. The schedule won't be like this when Nick is finished with the bookings," Val assured her, then grinned. "We both just thought you'd prefer to be close to home around the time the baby's due."

"I am not pregnant," Laurie repeated with a stubborn jut of her chin.

"Saying it won't make it true," Val taunted. "See a doctor, Laurie. Take a home pregnancy test. Do something before you drive both of us nuts."

She glanced up just then and spotted Annie standing hesitantly on the deck outside.

"Is it okay?" Annie whispered, her awestruck gaze fixed on Laurie, though the question was directed to Val.

"Of course it's okay," Val said. "Laurie, this is Annie Sutton."

"Hi," Annie said shyly, not budging from outside. "My dad said not to bother you, if you were busy."

"We're not busy," Laurie said. "More's the pity."

"You were singing before," Annie said. "I heard you. I hope that's okay."

Val wondered how much more Annie had heard before she'd made her presence known. Her expression, however, was totally innocent. Maybe she'd been so captivated just being near Laurie that she hadn't been paying any attention to the rest.

Laurie grinned at her. "What did you think of the song? Tell the truth. I can take it."

"I thought it was awesome, not as sad as what you usually do," Annie said, creeping inside. "Is it finished?"

"Not yet. I can't decide if I like it." Laurie studied Annie intently. "You really liked it, huh?"

Annie nodded. "Especially the part about finding someone new inside. I feel like that sometimes, as if I'm not who I was anymore, but I don't know yet who I am."

Val saw the sudden inspiration flare to life in Laurie's eyes. She grabbed her guitar off the sofa and began to toy with the lyrics that she'd been struggling with earlier. Annie crept closer and sat down to listen, her rapt gaze never leaving Laurie's face.

Time seemed to stand still as Laurie captured what Annie had so eloquently expressed, and turned it into the beginnings of a song. As the first words flowed, Val grabbed a pad and jotted them down. She knew from experience that Laurie would want to see them in black and white later. For now, she was too caught up in the creative process to take the time to make sure the words weren't lost as soon as they were uttered.

When the last notes faded away, Annie looked as if she'd been given a precious gift. "That's what I said," she whispered. "You sang what I said."

Laurie grinned. "You inspired it, all right. Thank you. I was stuck until you came in here."

"You mean I helped? I really helped?"

"More than you'll know," Val told her fervently. Maybe now Laurie would realize that the only block to her continued success was in her own mental attitude toward the future. "Now let's get out of here and let Laurie work in peace. She won't be happy until every note's perfect."

"I thought it sounded perfect just the way it was," Annie told her.

"Not yet," Laurie said. "But thanks to you, it's getting there."

Annie followed Val to the door with obvious reluctance. Just as they were about to go out, she turned back. "What's it called?"

"'Where'd I Go?'" Laurie told her. "But I'm going to think of it as Annie's song. And whenever I sing it, I'll tell the audience about the young lady who helped me write it."

"Oh, wow!" Annie murmured, eyes shining. "Wait till my dad hears about this." Outside, she gazed up at Val. "Do you think she really meant it? Will she put that song on an album? Will she really tell people about me?"

"She'll have to run it past some people, but I'd say yes. Laurie usually knows a hit when she hears it." Unwittingly, Annie had captured Laurie's own mood with her words. She'd given her an excuse for writing about the changes that scared Laurie to death. The meeting had been good for both of them. "As for telling her fans about you, Laurie always gives credit where it's due."

Val grinned down at Annie. "How about you and I go into town and celebrate? I'll buy you the biggest sundae they serve at Dolan's. Remember? That's the place I told you about. If we're lucky, Sharon Lynn will have her new baby there with her."

"Really? You can go now? You don't have to work or something?"

"I can go. Let's see if your dad says it's okay for you to come along."

Some of the light in Annie's eyes faded. "He won't care. He's working. I haven't seen him all day. He told me to stick close to home and not get into trouble."

"Ask him anyway," Val insisted. "He's probably at the stables. I'll wait at the car."

Annie gave her a put-upon look, but she scampered off dutifully. Val resisted the temptation to follow and make sure she actually talked to Slade. Annie needed to have someone trust her, and Val needed to learn to resist the urge to make excuses to catch a glimpse of Slade. It was way past time to try out a new strategy. Straightforward hadn't cut it. Maybe the old-fashioned way—playing elusive and hard-to-get—would work.

Annie came back waving a five-dollar bill. "He said okay, but he's treating."

Val was oddly pleased by the gesture. It could hardly be counted as a date, since he wasn't even coming along, but it would be the first thing Slade had ever given her. Too bad she couldn't preserve an ice cream sundae as a souvenir. Maybe she'd tuck that five-dollar bill into a scrapbook, instead.

Seeing Annie and Val with their heads together was enough to send goosebumps sliding down Slade's back. It had been occurring with distressing regularity ever since Annie's arrival earlier in the week.

Over dinner on Annie's first night, all Slade had heard was "Val said this" and "Val said that." He probably should have been grateful that Annie was talking to him at all, but all he could think about was the topic. He had enough trouble keeping his mind off Val without her name coming up every two seconds. Still, he'd gritted his teeth and listened to every word Annie had to say about this new friend she'd acquired.

"And she said she'd take me into town tomorrow," she'd said, her eyes bright with excitement. "There's this place, Dolan's, that has ice cream and hamburgers. It's owned by a lady named Sharon Lynn. You probably know her. Her dad's your boss or something. Anyway, Val said Dolan's is *the* place to go in Los Piños. Or she said we could go for pizza. It's not like one of those national chains. It's made by a real Italian family. I think they came from Rome way back even. Anyway, she said it's my choice. So, what do you think?"

What Slade thought was that the woman was as pesky as flies at a picnic. There hadn't been a single day since she'd first turned up at White Pines that she'd minded her own business. If she got it into her head to befriend Annie, it could only mean trouble. It would start with ice cream and pizza, but who knew where it would lead? Still, he couldn't bring himself to put a damper on Annie's enthusiasm by saying no.

"If you want to go, it's fine," he'd said. "Just don't take advantage. I'll give you the money for your food."

"No, it's her treat. She said so."

But when Annie had come to him for permission, he'd insisted on giving her the money for ice cream. A gentleman didn't let a lady pay. The lesson had been drilled into him by his mother and echoed by his father. It had stuck, which he supposed made him some kind of an old-fashioned oddity in this day and age of dutch treat and ladies doing the asking for dates. On the circuit he'd been astounded by just how brazen some women were, even once they knew he was married.

Annie and Val went for ice cream and burgers on Monday. They had pizza on Tuesday. Val planned a swim in the creek and a picnic on Wednesday. The two of them were thick as thieves. Yes, indeed, it made his skin crawl. Annie needed a new friend, one who wasn't old enough and sexy enough to make her daddy's heart pump quite so hard.

Kids her own age would be good, he concluded, and the ranch was crawling with them. Was it possible to arrange some sort of play date at Annie's age? He could talk to Cody about it. Or should he just pray that the kids found each other before hearing about Val drove him nuts?

The thought had barely occurred to him when he spotted Val striding toward him with a purposeful gleam in her eyes. Watching her walk was a thoroughly entertaining experience. The woman's hips swayed provocatively enough to make a man's blood steam, especially when she got the notion to wear a pair of kick-ass heels that made her legs look long and willowy, despite the fact that she was just a little bitty thing. She'd worn those heels today as if she knew the effect they had on him.

He indulged in a moment of purely masculine appreciation before he reminded himself that that expression on her face spelled upheaval.

"Whatever it is, the answer is no," he announced emphatically when she was several yards away. He turned his attention back to the horse he'd been grooming before he'd caught sight of Val.

When she remained silent for way too long, he risked a glance up. She gave him one of her irrepressible grins. "Good. I have your attention. Just for the record, I haven't asked for anything yet."

"But you will," he muttered. "You always do."

She laughed. "See, we are making progress. You already know me very well."

"That is not a blessing." he retorted.

"Oh, hush, and hear me out," she said, clearly undaunted. "I was thinking we ought to plan a little get-together in Annie's honor. She should get to know all the kids in the family. Not that I don't enjoy her company, because I do, but she needs to have friends her own age. I'm sure she has to be missing the ones she left behind."

Slade wanted to resist the idea just because it had come from Val, but she was right. He'd been thinking precisely the same thing not minutes ago, albeit for very different reasons. Like Val, though, he could see how much it would mean to his daughter to make some friends. Maybe they could fill in the gaps in her life that he couldn't. He couldn't go on relying on Val to keep Annie occupied indefinitely.

"Fine," he said grudgingly, relieved that she seemed to have some sort of a plan in mind. "Do whatever you want. I'll pay for it."

"Oh, no, you don't," she retorted. "Not me. *You and me,*" she said with emphasis. "This is a joint venture. I'll do the inviting, if you like, but you have to put out a little effort, too."

He regarded her warily. "Such as?"

"Make arrangements with Harlan to use the barbecue and pool up at the main house, plan a menu with Annie, then pick up the food from town. It'll mean the world to Annie that you want to do this for her."

He supposed she had a point. Gestures probably mattered to females of all ages. Suzanne had certainly counted on them. She'd expected flowers, candy or jewelry every time he'd walked through the door.

"Okay, I'll talk to Harlan," he agreed. "But I don't know a damn thing about planning a menu. I'm lucky if I get a frozen meal on the table for dinner without nuking it to death. Besides, in case you haven't noticed, Anne and I don't communicate real well."

Val regarded him with impatience. "Oh, for goodness sakes, how hard can it be for the two of you to put your heads together and come up with a standard barbecue menu? Steaks, burgers, potato salad, coleslaw, baked beans, dessert. How complicated is that?''

He grinned despite himself. If there was one thing he'd learned about Val Harding, it was that she was frighteningly efficient. ''Sounds to me like you've got it all worked out. We'll go with that.''

She looked as if she might argue, but she nodded instead. ''Okay, then. You set the date with Harlan, and then the three of us will go shopping. We'll make a day of it.''

He sighed, thinking of the number of Adamses involved and the likely expense. He had money in the bank from his rodeo days—at least what was left after Suzanne had taken a healthy share of his winnings. He'd been stashing away most of his salary to buy his own ranch sometime down the road. He intended to buy the best horses in Texas, then breed and train them. This little party clearly would put a serious crimp in that plan. The kind of blowout Val was describing cost big bucks. For something that lasted a few hours, it seemed like a waste of good money.

''Maybe we should think about hot dogs, instead. And kids like chips. Maybe some homemade ice cream.'' His enthusiasm mounted. ''Yeah, that would work.''

One look at Val's expression killed the idea.

''No way, Sutton. When it comes to entertaining, I believe in going all out. Bring your wallet. I only buy the best.''

"I was afraid of that," he said resignedly.

"Don't look so terrified. It'll only hurt for a little while." She winked. "And if you play your cards right, I'll kiss you and make it better."

Now there was a prospect that could take a man's mind off the agony of having his budget blown to smithereens. Unfortunately, it also conjured up images that made mincemeat out of all that restraint he'd been working so hard to hang on to.

"Maybe I should just write you a blank check and let you go for it," he suggested hopefully.

She gave him an amused, knowing look. "The prospect of spending the day in town with me doesn't scare you, does it?"

"Falling off the back of a two-thousand-pound, mean-spirited bull scares me. Getting trampled by a bucking bronc gives me pause. You..." he gave her a pointed look "...you're just a pesky little annoyance."

For an instant he thought he caught a flash of hurt in her eyes and regretted that he'd been the cause of it. He ignored the temptation to apologize, though. If he could get her to write him off as a jerk, maybe he'd finally get some peace.

Of course, then he'd also be all on his own with Annie. *That* was more terrifying than the bull, the bronc and Val all rolled into one.

"Sorry," he muttered halfheartedly.

"For what?" she said, her eyes shining a little too brightly. "Being honest? No one can fault you for that."

"Still, I should have kept my mouth shut. You've been good to my daughter. I owe you."

"Now that's where you're wrong. Around here people look out for one another, no thanks necessary."

"And where I come from, you don't lash out at someone who's done you a kindness."

A faint smile tugged at her lips. "Are we going to argue about this, too?"

Slade shrugged. He figured arguing was a whole lot safer than the kissing he was seriously tempted to do. "More than likely."

"Maybe we could call a truce," she suggested. "For Annie's sake."

"Won't work," he said succinctly.

"Why on earth not?"

"Well, now, the way I see it, you and I are destined to butt heads."

"Because that's the way you want it," she accused.

Slade grinned. "No, because you're a woman and I'm a man. Simple as that."

"Tell me something I didn't know. Why does that mean we have to fight?"

"Human nature."

"Sweetheart, if that were human nature, the population would dwindle down to nothing."

He gazed directly into her eyes, then quaked inside at the impact of that. Still, he managed to keep his voice steady. "Now, you see, *sweetheart,* that's where God steps in. He set it up so all that commotion would be counterbalanced by making up. Bingo, you've got babies."

Val listened to him, her eyes sparkling with growing amusement. When he'd finished, she grinned at him. "Seems to me like you've just given me something to look forward to, cowboy. Let me know anytime you're ready to start making up."

She turned then and sashayed off, leaving Slade to stare after her in openmouthed astonishment. Just when he thought he finally had her on the ropes, dadgumit, she won another round.

Chapter Four

Slade was just starting to check out a prized new stallion that had been delivered when he glanced up and saw Harlan Adams waiting just outside the stall, his gnarled hands curved over the top rail.

"Something I can do for you?" he asked the rancher. Slade had to wonder if this had something to do with the party. They'd already discussed it, and Harlan had embraced the idea with the expected enthusiasm.

Harlan Adams might have relinquished the day-to-day running of White Pines to Cody and Harlan Patrick, but no one who knew anything about him doubted the influence he still held over the place. Even in his eighties, his mind was sharp as a tack. Only the physical limitations of aging kept him from doing everything his son and grandson did. Slade always tried to grant him the respect he was due, even when the man hadn't just done him a huge favor.

"Just came down to get a look at that horse you and Cody spent a fortune of my hard-earned money on," he replied, his gaze moving over Black Knight as if he expected the horse to be nothing less than solid gold.

"We'll get some excellent foals for you in a year or two," Slade said. Even though Harlan's grumbling remark about the stallion's cost had been made goodnaturedly, Slade was unable to keep a hint of defensiveness out of his own voice. "He was worth every penny."

"Oh, he's a beauty, all right," Harlan agreed readily. "Don't get all lathered up, Son. I trust your judgment. Cody carried on so, I just wanted to see him for myself. Thought it might give us a chance to talk some more, too. You were in too big a hurry when you stopped by the house to ask about the party."

The casual announcement set off alarms. Harlan Adams never came out to the stables merely to chat. He came when he wanted to poke and pry into matters that were none of his concern. Slade waited warily to hear what was on his mind.

Harlan found a stool and dragged it over so he could observe as Slade expertly went over the horse. Not used to having anyone watch his every move—except when he'd been in the rodeo ring—Slade was unsettled by the intense scrutiny. His nervousness promptly communicated itself to the powerful stallion. Black Knight turned skittish, prancing dangerously close to the walls of his stall. Slade smoothed a hand over his flank and murmured to him until he settled down.

"You've got a way with these animals, don't you?" Harlan observed with apparent admiration. "Cody claims he's never seen anyone better."

Slade shrugged, though he was pleased by the compliment. "I suppose. I just treat 'em like the magnificent creatures they are."

"The way a man treats his stock says a lot about him, if you ask me." The rancher paused, then asked with disconcerting directness, "You as good with your daughter?"

Startled by the abrupt shift in subject to something so personal, Slade snapped his head up. Defensiveness had his stomach clenching again. "Meaning?"

Seemingly oblivious to the tension in Slade's voice, the old man pointed out, "You kept her hidden away long enough. Didn't even mention her when you applied for work. Never knew a man to hide the fact that he had family, especially a daughter as clever as your Annie. Why was that?"

"With all due respect, sir, I think that's my business."

Harlan Adams regarded him unrepentantly. "Well, of course it is. That doesn't mean I can't ask about it, does it? Around here, we like to think of the people working for us as part of the family. You've been here long enough to know when it comes to family, we tend to meddle. It's second nature to us."

Slade managed a halfhearted grin at that. "So I've heard." He just hadn't expected to become a target of it. It made him damned uncomfortable having to answer to his boss about his relationship with Annie. He doubted an outsider would understand all the complicated emotions at work.

"Well, then, tell me about your girl," Harlan prodded again, clearly not intending to let the matter drop. "She made a real good impression when I met her. Val brought her by the house for a visit the other day."

"What can I say, sir? She's a handful." A worrisome thought struck him. "She hasn't gotten into some sort of mischief around here already, has she?"

'Of course not," Harlan said, dismissing that worry. "We're glad to have her. She reminds me of my Jenny, the way she was when her mama and I first started going out. Whoo-ee, that girl was a hellion back then. Gave her mama and me fits. Not a one of my boys was as much trouble, and believe me, they weren't saints."

"Is that so?" Slade doubted Jenny Adams had ever gotten into the kind of mischief Annie could pull off.

"Stole my truck, for starters," Harlan told him.

Slade stared, thinking of the beautiful, self-possessed young woman he'd met at ranch gatherings. He could think of a lot of ways to describe Jenny, but car thief wouldn't have been among them. She'd been an activist for Native American affairs. Now she taught school and was darn good at it, from what he'd heard. A bit unconventional, perhaps, but effective.

"You're kidding me," he said, sure the old man had to be pulling his leg to make him feel better about Annie's misdeeds.

"No, indeed. Girl was just fourteen, too. Smacked the truck straight into a tree." He almost sounded proud of her accomplishment.

"I take it she wasn't hurt," Slade said.

"No, thank the Lord. When I caught up with her, she was cursing a blue streak, like the car was to blame. I brought her back into town to face the music. That's how I met her mama. Janet had just opened up her law practice here in town. Jenny was none too pleased about her mama's divorce or about being uprooted from New York. She was mad at the world. I brought her out here and put her to work. She tended to be mischievous like your Annie, to put a generous spin on it." A grin spread across his face. "Took a paintbrush to some of the buildings around here, too. I never saw such a mess."

Slade shook his head, baffled by Harlan's amused expression as he told the story. "And you and Janet still got married? Amazing."

"Nothing amazing about it. Janet and I were suited. I could see that right from the start, though it took a little longer to bring her around to my way of thinking," he said. "As for Jenny, she came around, too, once she knew I'd go on loving her no matter what she did. Persistence, that's the ticket. Something you ought to remember. It's a trait to value."

Slade didn't ask why. He was afraid he knew, and it didn't have a thing to do with his relationship with Annie. An image of Val flitted through his mind. That woman could write the book on persistence.

Harlan clearly wasn't through doling out advice. "You know, Son, a little spirit in a girl's a good thing, especially in this day and age. A woman needs to know how to stand up for herself. How else is she supposed to learn that without testing her wings as a kid?''

He grinned. ''Besides, most always what goes around, comes around. Being reminded of that gets you through the bad times. Jenny certainly got her comeuppance in due time. She's a teacher now and a stepmom to a little hellion herself. She's getting all that trouble back in spades. Knows how to handle it, though, because she's been there herself.''

''Maybe I should send Annie over to you to raise,'' Slade said, only partly in jest. ''You sound far better equipped to cope with her than I am.''

''Oh, I suspect you'll get the hang of it soon enough. In the meantime, you've got a pretty little stand-in,'' he said, his expression sly. ''Val seems to be taking quite an interest in Annie. In you, too, from what I've observed.''

Slade had no intention in discussing his love life—or lack thereof—with Harlan Adams. In addition to meddling for the sheer pleasure of it, the man was the sneakiest matchmaker in Texas. Prided himself on it, in fact.

''Val's been very kind to Annie,'' Slade agreed, and left it at that. ''So have you. Thank you again for agreeing to this party. It'll go a long way toward making her feel more at home here.''

''That's what a ranch like this is meant for,'' Harlan said. ''What's the fun in living to a ripe old age, if you can't surround yourself with family and lots of young people? I'm looking forward to seeing 'em all splashing around in that big old pool out back. Plus it gives me a chance to hear Laurie sing. Nobody has a voice like Harlan Patrick's wife. Millions of folks pay to hear her concerts, but I can usually coax her into singing a song or two just for family. Gives me pleasure.''

"I'm sure it does.''

"I heard she wrote a song for Annie.''

Slade was taken aback by that. "Are you sure about that?''

"First day they met, the way I hear it. Annie gave her the inspiration.''

"Imagine that,'' Slade murmured. Annie must have been over the moon, but she hadn't said a word.

Or maybe—as happened all too often—he just hadn't been listening.

As Harlan Adams headed back up to the main house, Slade stared after him, then sighed. He had a feeling this was one time when the old man had been just as clever about passing along advice as he usually was about digging out secrets or meddling in affairs of the heart. He'd probably be keeping a close eye out to see just how well Slade followed it.

Val was in her element pulling the party together. Nothing gave her a sense of accomplishment like making lists and checking off every little chore. She'd helped Laurie with enough entertaining that it was second nature to her. This party would be smaller and less formal than something Laurie would have thrown in Nashville, but the details were essentially the same.

She enlisted Annie's help, thoroughly enjoying the

child's wry sense of humor, which came out at the most unexpected moments, shattering that tough, sullen facade she wore the rest of the time. Then there were the rare moments of vulnerability that tore at Val's heart.

"What if the kids don't like me?" Annie asked for the millionth time a few days before the barbecue.

"They'll like you," Val reassured her. "Dani's twins are about your age, but most of the others are younger. You'll be like a big sister to them. They'll look up to you. Look how well you get along with Amy Lynn. She toddles around after you like a puppy."

"What does she know?" Annie scoffed. "She's just a baby."

"The point is, she likes you just fine. So will all the others."

"They'll make fun of me."

"Why on earth would they make fun of you?" Val asked.

"For one thing, my hair's a mess."

"The cut is a little uneven, that's all," Val insisted in what had to be the most massive understatement she'd ever made in the name of kindness. She'd gathered that Annie had done the style herself in a fit of anger over being sent to live with her father. "I could try to trim it a little more evenly, if you like."

Annie's eyes brightened. "Could you?"

"I'll take a shot at it, unless you'd prefer to get it cut in town."

Annie shook her head. "My dad would never pay

for it. He'd say it was a waste of money to fix something I did to myself in the first place.''

Val had a feeling they had already had exactly that discussion. She couldn't honestly say she blamed Slade. Still, Annie had probably suffered long enough for her ill-conceived moment of rebellion.

"I'll get the scissors. You go and wash your hair," she told Annie. Beyond shaving the child's head, she doubted there was anything she could do that could possibly make her hairstyle worse than it was.

Fortunately, Annie had a little curl to her hair and the delicately shaped face of a pixie. Val snipped and trimmed until her hair was short as a boy's. The curl softened the effect, feathering against her cheek and drawing attention to her lovely green eyes. Val stood back and surveyed the results.

"I think you look beautiful, if I do say so myself," she said, handing Annie a mirror. "You have the perfect face for a style this short. Those gorgeous eyes of yours look huge. You are going to be a heartbreaker one of these days, young lady."

"No way," Annie said, then took the mirror Val held out. She gazed into it, then up at Val. "I'm almost pretty," she whispered in an awestruck voice.

"Well, of course you're pretty," Val said, glad she'd been able to take away one of Annie's worries.

"But what will I wear?" Annie moaned now. "All I have is a ratty old bathing suit that's too small. You saw it the day we went to the creek. I can't wear that."

Val had to concede it no longer fit and had been faded by too much sun and chlorine from the town pool in Wilder's Glen. "I'll bet if you explain that to your dad, he'll let you get a new one."

Annie looked defeated. "He won't go for it." She glanced up at Val hopefully. "Maybe you could ask him. He'll listen to you."

"No," Val insisted. "You discuss it with him."

"He doesn't listen to a word I say," Annie grumbled. "Did you know I told him about Laurie writing a song for me? He mumbled something that sounded like 'that's nice,' then went right on reading a bunch of old horse magazines."

"Obviously you picked a bad time."

"It's *always* a bad time," Annie complained. "I'm always interrupting something more important."

Val vowed to speak to Slade about paying more attention when his daughter tried to have a conversation with him.

"I wish I were your daughter," Annie said with a heavy sigh. "You listen to me all the time."

"That's because when you and I are together, you have my undivided attention. If you tried to talk to me when I'm working, I probably would be every bit as distracted as your dad. Lesson one, kiddo, if you want something from someone, make sure it's a good time before you ask, otherwise the answer will be no for sure."

"How can you tell?"

"Instinct."

"I don't think I have that," Annie said glumly.

Val chuckled. "You will. It takes time to develop. You're only ten. It just means being more sensitive to other people's moods."

"Like if my dad's worried about some old horse or something, I shouldn't ask him for something," Annie said, her expression thoughtful.

"Exactly. Either leave him alone or ask about the horse. Sympathize with him."

"Okay, I get it." She jumped off the kitchen chair and headed for the door. "Bye. Thanks for the haircut."

"You're welcome. Where are you off to?"

"I'm going to see if my dad's in a good mood or not so I can ask about the bathing suit." Her step faltered. "If he's in a bad mood, do you think you could help me bake him chocolate chip cookies? Those are his favorites. He's bound to listen to me after that."

"See if you can't pull it off using your wits," Val said. "But, yes, if all else fails, I'll help with the cookies."

So, she thought after Annie was gone, chocolate was the way to Slade's heart. She just happened to have a recipe for a chocolate cake that had been known to bring grown men to their knees. It might be just the dessert to serve at Annie's party. She would personally see to it that Slade got a very large slice.

Slade gave Val a pleading look on Friday afternoon when she turned up at the stables to remind him they had to go into town to shop for the party. He reached into his pocket and started to peel off a wad of bills.

"Can't you and Annie go? I've got work to do." He held out the cash.

Val ignored it and met his gaze evenly. "No."

Slade blinked. "No? Just like that? You won't even consider it?"

"No," she repeated. "Just like that. Annie and I have done all the planning up until now. The deal was that we would all go shopping. I'm not letting you renege."

"I told her she could buy a bathing suit if you helped to pick it out," he said, as if that might convince her of his honorable intentions.

He could have saved his breath. Val had an agenda here and she didn't intend to be deterred. "That's very generous of you. She really needs one." She grinned. "But you're not getting off the hook by throwing more money our way. She needs to spend time with you, too."

"I guarantee she'd have more fun if the two of you went without me," Slade said.

"Could be," Val agreed readily. "Unless you work really hard at getting through to her."

He gave her a sour look. "Lady, you drive a really hard bargain."

She nodded unrepentently. "That's why Laurie pays me the big bucks. And just so you know, thanks to her, I have lots of practice at getting my way." She winked at him. "Five minutes, cowboy. We'll meet you at the car."

Slade turned up five minutes later, still looking none too pleased. After a disconcerted glance at Val, who was already behind the wheel, he climbed into the passenger seat with obvious reluctance.

"Everybody belted up?" Val inquired pointedly.

Slade heaved a sigh and put on his seat belt.

She grinned at him. "Thank you."

"No problem."

She had already made a mental list of possible topics to try to get Slade and Annie talking. By the time they reached town, she had exhausted most of them, right along with her nerves. It had been the most frustrating half hour of her life. Slade answered in monosyllables. Apparently picking up on her father's mood, Annie retreated into sullen silence.

"What shall we do first?" Val asked when she'd parked on the main street in Los Piños. She turned to Annie. "Shall we try to find a bathing suit?"

"Whatever," Annie said.

Undaunted, Val led her scowling companions to the general store, one of the few places in town that carried clothes and the only one that carried bathing suits. The selection wouldn't be the greatest, but she doubted she could have coerced Slade or Annie into going over to Garden City instead. They obviously didn't want to spend one more minute in each other's company than they had to.

Because Annie was dragging her feet and Slade looked as uncomfortable as if she'd coaxed him unwittingly into a lingerie shop, Val seized the initiative. She selected several bathing suits in various styles from the rack and held them up for Annie's inspection.

"That one, I guess," Annie said without enthusiasm, pointing at a bright red one-piece suit.

Val held it up for Slade's approval. "What do you think?"

"Whatever Annie wants."

Val wanted to shake the pair of them. "Well, I like the green," she said instead. "It's the color of your eyes. Try them both on," she instructed, handing them to Annie.

When the girl had gone off to the dressing room, Val whirled on Slade. "Could you possibly manage to show just a little enthusiasm? You're acting as if this is a worse chore than mucking out stalls."

Something that might have been guilt flickered in his eyes. He sighed. "Okay, you're right. I'm being a pain in the butt."

"Any particular reason or is this just your general nature?"

"Shopping's not my thing, okay? I don't know what she should get."

"Then, unless it is totally inappropriate, let her pick what she likes."

"How am I supposed to know that? She looked pretty miserable no matter which one you held up."

"That's because she's reacting to your mood. Now when she comes back out here, give her a compliment. Tell her she looks great. Tell her she looks grown-up. Just show some enthusiasm. Fake it, if you have to."

He regarded her with unexpected amusement. "You're recommending that I lie to my daughter? You, the queen of directness, are suggesting that I fib?"

"As a general rule, a lie is not the answer, but some situations call for drastic measures," she retorted. She glanced up and saw Annie standing hesitantly just outside the curtain of the dressing room. The red suit that Annie had liked best was clearly intended for someone who actually had a bust. Val swallowed hard at the sight, then muttered so only Slade could hear, "This is one of them."

She could see him struggling with a smile, but he managed to say cheerfully, "That suit's real bright, honey. Is it the one you want?"

Annie's gaze faltered. "I'm not so sure. It's kinda big." She gestured. "Up here."

"Too big," Val said decisively, greatly relieved that Annie had voiced it first. "Try the other one."

When Annie had retreated to the dressing room, Slade glanced over at Val. "So. tell me, what happened to the little white lie?"

"You gave her moral support. I gave her the truth," she replied. "It balances out."

"You could give her both and I could keep my mouth shut," Slade suggested. "I don't seem to be getting the rules. Or is it that you keep changing them?"

Val frowned at him. "You really don't have much instinct for this sort of thing, do you?"

"Not a bit," he agreed without remorse.

"Well, you're just going to have to learn," she said decisively. "And now's your chance."

Annie reappeared in the green bathing suit. It was a perfect fit. "How about this one?" she asked, glancing hopefully straight at her father.

He surveyed her intently, then gestured for her to turn around. She did a slow pirouette and then he nodded. "Real flattering," he said at last, the compliment all the more meaningful because he had clearly struggled for it. "You'll glide through the water like a little fish in that."

As compliments went, it wasn't all that pretty, and he looked awkward as the dickens as he said it, but Val had to give him points for trying. As for Annie, she looked as if he'd just told her she looked like a princess.

"You used to say that to me a long time ago, didn't you?" she asked shyly. "That I could swim like a fish?"

Slade appeared startled, then a slow smile spread across his face. "You couldn't have been much more than a baby back then. I took you down to the pool when we were on a visit to your grandmama's." He regarded her with amazement. "You actually remember that?"

"I remember a lot," she said, her eyes suddenly glistening with unshed tears. Then she spun away and ran to the dressing room.

Slade gazed helplessly at Val. "What did I say wrong?"

She reached up and touched a hand to his cheek. "Nothing. For once, I think you got it just right."

"But she's crying."

"Because you connected with her. You shared a memory, made her see that there was a time in the past when something you did together was as special to you as it was to her."

Slade shook his head, still staring after Annie, his expression miserable. "I never could stand to see her cry."

Val tucked that little tidbit away right next to his secret addiction to chocolate. She was beginning to discover that despite his gruff, tough exterior, Slade Sutton was an old softie, after all. It made her more determined than ever to snag him for herself.

Chapter Five

When Annie finally reappeared, clutching the green bathing suit, her eyes were puffy from crying. Slade's first instinct was to gather her in his arms as he would have when she was a toddler. It had been so long, though, that he was afraid she'd rebuff the gesture.

"Let's pay for this and get some lunch," he suggested instead. "I vote for pizza."

He was rewarded with the faintest glimmer of a smile on Annie's face. He grinned back at her. "Still your favorite?"

"With pepperoni and sausage," she said.

"What about anchovies?" he teased.

"No way you're putting little fishies on my pizza. If you want 'em, get your own."

He turned to Val. "And you? Can I talk you into anchovies?"

"Not a chance."

He feigned a disappointed sigh. "I guess I'll just have to make the sacrifice and go with pepperoni and sausage."

Annie regarded him wisely. "You never get anchovies. I don't think you really like them."

"Well, of course I do," he insisted. "Biggest sacrifice of my life, giving up those little fishies."

"Then get your own pizza," Val suggested, winking at Annie. "She and I can share."

"Yeah, Daddy. Why don't you get your own and have it just the way you like it?"

"Nope. Can't eat a whole one. I'll just have what you guys are having."

Val gave Annie a knowing look. "Yep, you're right. He's faking it."

Just to prove them wrong, he ordered anchovies on two slices of their large pizza and forced himself not to gag while he took the first bite.

"Best I ever had," he claimed as he finished the first piece.

Annie watched him intently, then reached for the second slice. "Let me try it." She bit into it, then grimaced. "Oh, yuck. How can you eat that?"

"Because we all but dared him to," Val said. "Some men will do anything if they're challenged."

"Is that it, Daddy?" Annie asked skeptically. "Was it just because we dared you?"

"Okay, yes," he said finally, his gaze locked with Val's. "You caught me."

Annie grinned, apparently satisfied that her first instincts about the anchovies had been accurate. "You don't have to eat the other slice. You can have some of ours.''

"Oh, I don't know about that," Val chimed in, a wicked gleam in her eyes. "I think he should finish what he started. Wasting good food's a crime, when so many people around the world are starving."

"I'll mail the leftover slice of pizza to anyone you care to suggest," he responded, already reaching for one of the more appetizing wedges. Val snagged his wrist in a grip that suggested, for a pipsqueak, she'd been doing some strength training in Laurie's home gym. "I take it you object."

"Oh, yes," she said. "That pizza has my name on it."

He leaned over and pretended to study it intently. "I can't see it. Can you, Annie?"

His daughter stood up and glanced at the slice carefully. "It's Val's, all right," she said at last.

His head snapped up. "You took her side," he said, genuinely bemused by it. "What kind of kid takes the side of a stranger over her own father?"

Though he'd said it in jest, as soon as the words were out of his mouth, he could see Annie's expression clouding over. He'd done it again—spoiled the mood for reasons that escaped him.

"Annie?" he prodded gently. "What did I say?"

"Nothing," she mumbled. "May I be excused?"

Slade noticed that she addressed the question to Val.

Looking troubled, Val asked, "Where will you be?"

"Outside, I guess."

"Slade?" Val said, turning to him.

"Fine, go," he said tersely. When Annie had left, he scowled at Val. "Okay, I blew it again. Mind telling me how?"

"You all but told her that, for siding with me, she wasn't a good kid," she said. "I know you were teasing, but she took it to heart."

"Are you telling me that every time I open my mouth, I'm going to be walking through a minefield?"

She nodded. "Pretty much."

"Which one of us do you think is going to crack first?" he asked.

"My money's on you, unless you can learn to roll with it. Think about this," she said with a certain amount of glee. "Puberty's going to be much, much worse."

Slade held up a hand. "Don't even say it."

"People survive it," Val assured him. "Kids and their parents."

"Maybe if there are two parents, who can bolster each other's spirits," he said.

"Oh, no, single moms survive it, too. Mine did."

Startled, he studied her face, saw the unexpected shadows in eyes that usually glinted with good humor. "Where was your dad?"

"He died when I was eight."

Which explained why she empathized with Annie, why she was fighting like a tigress to see that the lines of communications between him and his daughter were opened. No doubt it pained her to see a child with a perfectly good, healthy father going through life as if she had none.

"I'm sorry," Slade said. "That must have been tough."

"It was." Her expression turned from sad to thoughtful. "Funny, I've lived most of my life without him, yet I still miss him. I can still remember the scent of his pipe tobacco, the way it felt when he scooped me up and hugged me. I felt such a sense of security, as if no harm could ever come to me. After that, there were just years and years of uncertainty, even though my mom was terrific and worked her butt off for us."

She shook her head, as if clearing it of unwanted memories. "Sorry. We were talking about you and Annie."

Slade nodded. "Yes. I think we were. That's why you care so deeply what happens between her and me, isn't it?"

She seemed surprised by the suggestion. "I hadn't thought about it, but, yes, I suppose it's one reason. I wouldn't have expected you to pick up on that."

"Because I'm just an insensitive jerk?"

"Some of the time," she agreed bluntly.

Her gaze met his with that directness he sometimes found so disconcerting.

"Other times you can be…surprising," she added.

"You said your past might be only one of the reasons my relationship with my daughter matters to you. What's another?"

"Maybe I'm just a sucker for a happy ending."

Slade had the feeling that it was a whole lot more

complicated than that, more personal. He'd known from the beginning that she was attracted to him, but he'd figured his refusal to get involved had only turned him into a challenge. Now he wondered if he'd been wrong. Could she be developing real feelings for him? He hoped not. He could have told her he was a bad bet. Hell, she could surely see that for herself after all these months.

Finally, he dragged his gaze away from hers, tried to ignore the rock-hard arousal that long, lingering glance had stirred. If he'd been a different kind of man or she'd been a different kind of woman, maybe they could have done something about it. As it was, she was off-limits.

"We should probably be going," he said, his voice gruffer than he intended. He busied himself with calling for the bill, carefully counting out the money, taking enough time to assure that his body settled down.

When he finally risked another look at Val, the color was still high in her cheeks, as if she were embarrassed at unwittingly revealing some innermost secret.

"Ready?" he asked.

"Sure," she said, her controlled facade slipping neatly back into place. She moved briskly from the restaurant, allowing him no more than a glimpse of that swaying walk of hers. Just outside the door, she halted abruptly.

"What's wrong?" Slade asked.

Val glanced up and down the street. "I don't see

any sign of Annie. She promised to stay right out here and she's gone.''

"She's probably just popped into one of the stores,'' Slade said, stepping out onto the sidewalk to see for himself. "Come on, let's check Dolan's. She seems to have developed a real fondness for the ice cream there. She's probably trying to talk Sharon Lynn into giving her a cone right now.''

But Annie wasn't at the drugstore soda fountain and Sharon Lynn said she hadn't seen her.

"I had a bad feeling when she asked to go outside,'' Val said. "She was upset. I should have stopped her.''

"What about me? I'm her father. I didn't think she'd take off. Let's take a minute and think about this. It's a small town,'' he said, as much to reassure himself as Val. "How far could she have gone? It's been less than a half hour since she left the restaurant.''

He thought of the tale Harlan Adams had told him about Jenny. Surely he hadn't shared the same story with Annie. If so, was she impetuous enough to have tried the same stunt herself?

"Is the car still where we parked it?'' he asked, peering down the street.

"Well, of course,'' Val said, without even looking. "She can't drive, Slade.'' She dangled the keys in front of him. "I have these.''

He breathed a sigh of relief. It was one less thing to worry about. He doubted Annie's skills ran to hotwiring a car, unless she'd been hanging out at his father's garage. Still, he couldn't prevent the gut-sick sense of dread that washed through him when he realized that Annie was definitely missing.

Even though he'd just let her off the hook—and rightly so—he still wanted to rail at Val for getting them into this fix in the first place. If they hadn't been planning a party, if they hadn't come into town, if, if, if...

Bottom line, though, he had to find his daughter, and when he did, he was going to tan her hide, no matter what the so-called experts had to say about spanking these days.

For the next twenty minutes, he and Val searched high and low, but there was no sign of Annie in any of the likely places.

"You don't suppose she's gone to the bus station?" he asked Val, not quite able to bring himself to believe that his daughter was upset enough to truly run away. Had she decided to go back to his parents in Wilder's Glen? Could she possibly have enough money in her pocket for the ticket?

Val gave his hand a reassuring squeeze. "Stop it right this minute. That child adores you. She's not going to run away. All she really wants is your attention. She learned that misbehaving guaranteed that somebody would take notice. She's going to test you the same way she did her grandparents."

"That all sounds very logical, but she's a kid. Do you really think she's plotting this out in a reasonable manner?"

"No. It's instinctive with her. The best way to make sure you pay attention is to infuriate you."

Slade regarded her with impatience. "Didn't you

tell me not a half hour ago that she ran out because I hinted she wasn't a good kid? Why would she deliberately do something to prove just how bad she can be?''

"Because any attention is better than none."

"I've just spent the whole blasted day with her," Slade all but shouted in frustration.

Val touched his arm in a soothing gesture. "Slade, she's ten. It doesn't have to make sense. Come on. This is no time to panic. Let's settle down and think about this for a second. Where would she go?"

"We've looked at Dolan's. You've already looked at the pet shop, the toy store and the general store. I've been to the bookstore and the hardware store."

Val stared at him. "Why on earth would you think to look in a hardware store?"

"She likes tools." He shrugged. "Don't ask me why."

"Could be she's trying to be like you," Val said thoughtfully. "In which case, what about the feed and grain store? Did you look there?"

"She's never lived on a ranch before. Why would she go to a feed and grain store?"

"For the same reason she'd go to the hardware store—because it's something that interests you."

Slade didn't believe for an instant that they would find Annie standing amid bags of oats, but by golly, there she was, and she was rubbing her hand over a saddle with a look of pure longing on her face.

"Don't you dare yell at her," Val warned.

"I wasn't going to yell," Slade insisted, though he very likely would have if Val hadn't grabbed his arm and slowed him down. He took a deep breath, then shot a look at Val that apparently reassured her. She released his arm. He slowly crossed the store to stand beside his daughter.

"Hey, short stuff, we've been looking everywhere for you."

Her expression guilty, Annie snatched her hand away from the saddle. "I just figured you'd turn up here sooner or later," she said defensively.

"You could have said something to us before you took off," he suggested mildly. "You promised to wait just outside the restaurant."

"I guess I forgot about it." She gave him a defiant look. "Sort of like you broke your promise and didn't think to say goodbye when you took off and left me at Grandma's."

Slade was shocked by the accusation, especially since she'd obviously kept it bottled up inside for months now. "Of course I said goodbye. And we talked about you staying there while I went to look for work."

She shook her head. "You talked. I never agreed. When I got up in the morning, you were gone."

He thought back to that time and how little clear thinking he had been doing, and realized it was entirely possible that it had happened just that way. "I'm sorry."

She shrugged. "Yeah, well, it doesn't matter."

He hunkered down and took her by the shoulders. "Yes, it does matter, and I am sorry. I never meant to hurt you. I thought staying with Grandma would be the best thing for you."

"And you're the grown-up, so I guess that means you were right." She shrugged away from him. "Never mind. You found me now. Is it time to go home?"

Slade directed a helpless look in Val's direction and she immediately stepped in.

"We still have to buy food for the party," she reminded them. "That's why we came into town, remember?"

"I don't care about the party," Annie replied.

Slade was losing his fragile grip on his patience. "Fine," he said tightly. "We can always cancel."

Annie's alarmed gaze shot to his. "We can't call everyone and tell them to stay home."

He softened his tone. "Why not?"

"It would be rude." She turned to Val. "Wouldn't it?"

"Very rude," she agreed.

Relieved to see Annie's spirit returning, he nodded. "Then, by all means, let's go shopping."

The trip through the grocery store was an adventure. Slade should have known Val would come prepared. She had a mile-long list, organized precisely according to the aisles of the store. He was relegated to pushing the cart, while she and Annie made their selections with as much care as if they were choosing lifelong mates. Deciding which mustard to buy took on the significance of selecting the perfect present. He would have chosen the cheapest of everything and been out of the store in ten minutes. Annie and Val seemed to have very definite—and often diametrically opposed—opinions. They'd been debating white sweet corn versus yellow for the past five minutes.

"Slade, what do you think?"

"Corn's corn," he said.

"No, Daddy. Silver Queen is the best. Grandma says so."

"And I've always liked sweet yellow corn," Val said.

"Get some of each."

"A compromise," Val said, beaming at him as if he'd single-handedly brought peace to the Middle East. "What a novel idea."

"How much longer is this going to take?" he grumbled. "I have chores to do."

"Harlan Patrick said not to worry about the chores," Val informed him. "He said he'd take care of them."

Slade scowled. "You asked Harlan Patrick to take on my chores?"

"Settle down, cowboy. He volunteered. He knew we were going to be getting ready for the party. If you're going to follow us around with a scowl on your face, you might as well wait in the car."

He stared hard at her. She was serious. She was dismissing him as if he were an unruly kid.

"Can't do it. You need me to pay for all of this."

"I'll pay," she said, facing him stubbornly. "You can pay me back."

"If I'm forking out all this money, I want to see what I'm getting," he insisted.

"Fine. Suit yourself."

"I will."

Annie watched them intently, then sighed. "It's my fault, isn't it?"

"What's your fault?" he and Val demanded in a shocked chorus.

"That you're fighting. You probably never fought till I came."

"We barely spoke till you came," Val said with sincerity. "Don't worry about it, Annie. Your father and I are used to it. This is the way we communicate."

She tucked Annie's arm through hers. "Let's check out the steaks. I want really thick ones. How about you?"

"Daddy likes thick steaks, too," Annie said, as if trying to convince Val of their compatibility.

"Give it up, sweetie. Making peace between us is not your job," Val assured her, then leaned down to whisper something that had Annie grinning.

They moved off to the meat section, giggling. Slade watched them with their heads together and sighed heavily. Would he ever have that kind of easy relationship with Annie again? Or had he ruined it forever by abandoning her at her grandparents?

She and Val were still laughing when he found them loading up on steaks. As he got closer, he realized they were talking about dresses, of all things. Judging from Annie's recent wardrobe choices, he hadn't imagined she knew what a dress was. Val gave him a wink.

"Your daughter and I were just discussing whether or not we should get new outfits for the party. After all, we can't spend the whole day in bathing suits. What do you think?''

What he thought was that his entire life savings were going into this party. But even he was smart enough not to say that.

''I say go for it, if it's what you want.''

''Will you help us pick them out?'' Val inquired with a glint in her eyes that made him very uneasy.

''Me? In a dress shop? I don't know.'' The quest for a bathing suit had been disconcerting enough. He'd reduced his daughter to tears over that.

''Maybe I should just wait in the car,'' he suggested. ''And you can't take too long because we'll have all this food. It'll spoil in this heat.''

''Come on, Daddy. Please?'' Annie said.

It was the first time in a long time that she'd actually asked him for anything. After what she'd said earlier about him running out on her, how could he refuse?

Which was why he ended up spending the most unnerving two hours of his life sitting on a puffy yellow ottoman surrounded by frills and watching two females parade around in silk and satin that was more suited to a formal event than a barbecue. He got the feeling that they were just having fun playing dress-up.

Watching his daughter was one thing. Watching Val was something else entirely. The woman made very sure that she ratcheted his temperature up to white-hot before she showed an ounce of mercy. One of these days he'd make her pay for that, and he was getting some fascinating ideas about how.

"Have you two decided yet?" he asked eventually. "The steaks will be barbecued in the car pretty soon."

"One more dress," Annie pleaded.

"One more," he agreed.

When she came out of the dressing room this time she was wearing a yellow gingham sundress. She twirled around and made the skirt spin. "I like this one, Daddy. What do you think?"

"I think you'll be the prettiest girl at the party," he said, earning a beaming smile from Val, who'd already paid for her own selection.

He told himself that his effort to say the right thing had been made on Annie's behalf, but Val's approval touched something deep inside him. It had been a long time since what anyone thought had mattered. Maybe he was going to survive Suzanne's betrayal whether he wanted to or not.

Chapter Six

It never ceased to amaze Val how many members of the Adams family could be assembled at the drop of a hat. At the mention of a party, they swarmed to White Pines like ants getting word of a particularly tasty picnic. Even Luke and Jessie, who lived across the state, and their daughter Angela, who lived in Montana with her family, made it to White Pines for most events.

Harlan Adams was in his element presiding over this latest party. His grandchildren and great-grandchildren gravitated to him, not just because he was the family patriarch, but because of the love that flowed from him as tangibly as water splashing from a fountain.

It broke Val's heart to see Annie standing on the

fringes, looking left out. She knew if she'd been a little closer, she would have been able to detect the sheen of unshed tears in her eyes. Harlan, ever the thoughtful host, apparently spotted her about the same time.

"Well, there she is," he said, smiling warmly and beckoning to her. "Annie, my girl, come over here and meet the rest of these hellions. This is your party. You can't be standing on the sidelines."

Annie's expression brightened at once as she was introduced to various Adams cousins. Within minutes she and Jenny's stepson had teamed up against Dani's twin stepsons for a boisterous game of Marco Polo in the pool.

"She looks happy," Slade observed, sneaking up beside Val.

She turned and caught his sober expression. "She does, doesn't she?"

"Thank you for that."

"I didn't do anything."

"Don't be so modest," he chided. "You dreamed up this party and badgered me into it. You planned the guest list. You saw to it that Annie had the right things to wear. You bought the groceries."

"It's just a party, Slade," she said, reluctant to take too much credit for instigating such a simple thing.

He shook his head. "It's more than that, and you know it. It's a chance for Annie to make friends. You cared about her feelings, Val. I'm still not entirely certain why, but you did, and I'm grateful."

For some reason she couldn't explain, his thanks irked her. She told herself that he'd say the same if she'd been a hired caterer whose cheese puffs were especially tasty. "I don't want your gratitude," she said, though she was unable to explain just what she did want.

"A gracious woman would accept it, though." He grinned knowingly. "Any particular reason you're not? Are you holding out for something more?"

He had her pegged, she realized unhappily. Maybe what she wanted was as simple—or as monumental— as recognition that she could make a difference in his family, that she could fit in. She wanted him to see her in a new light, to realize what she could bring to his life.

Okay, she really wanted him to fall madly in love with her. And all because she'd helped him buy some clothes for his kid, and picked out some steaks. Was she crazy or what? Relationships didn't blossom based on a grand gesture.

"I'm sorry," she murmured. "I'm glad you're pleased with the way this turned out."

"I'd be even more pleased if you'd come eat with me," he said.

Val was astonished. It was rare for Slade to seek out her company. She usually had to throw herself at him. "Why?" she asked, regarding him warily.

"Why not?" he said, as if he uttered similar invitations all the time. "If you turn me down, I'll just end up talking horses all afternoon with Cody or Harlan Patrick. I can do that anytime."

She grinned. "I thought you liked nothing better than talking about horses."

"No, darlin', even I get tired of hearing my own

voice on that topic sometimes. Besides, only a fool would rather talk to a bunch of cowboys instead of a beautiful woman.''

She gazed into his eyes and saw a glimmer of amusement that was as rare as the invitation. ''Are you actually flirting with me?'' she asked, not bothering to hide her astonishment.

He leaned down to whisper in her ear. ''To tell the truth, it's been so long, I can't say for sure.''

The soft sigh of his breath across her cheek was almost as heady as a kiss. It made Val want to move an inch or two closer, to coax his arms around her. She'd been wanting him to kiss her for so long now she was just about ready to make it happen and damn the consequences.

''Maybe if you have a little food, you'll know for sure,'' she said, turning and leading the way to the buffet that she had helped the housekeeper set out earlier. ''Do you want the whole meal now or just an appetizer?'' She turned to find his gaze locked on her.

''An appetizer,'' he said quietly. ''Some things shouldn't be rushed.''

He really was flirting with her, she concluded. What she couldn't figure out was why. Not twenty-four hours ago he couldn't get away from her fast enough. Was it the party atmosphere? She hadn't noticed that his personality changed all that much at past parties. She regarded him suspiciously.

''What's really going on here, Slade?''

He looked as innocent as a newborn. ''I have no idea what you mean. I thought we'd grab some food, find a place away from the ruckus and enjoy some quiet conversation. Does that bother you for some reason?''

''Of course it doesn't bother me,'' she retorted. ''It's just so…out of character.''

''Maybe I've reformed.''

''Overnight?''

''They say the love of a good woman can do amazing things to change a man.''

She plunked down her plate. ''Okay, that's it. Who said anything about love?'' Her gaze narrowed. ''Has Laurie said something to you?''

''About?''

''Me, dammit.''

Laughter danced in his eyes. ''Can't say that I've talked to Laurie recently.''

As her temper lathered up, his grew cooler, Val noticed. It was very irksome. She tried to match his calm, even tone. ''Harlan Patrick, then.''

He grinned. ''Val, I don't know why you're making such a fuss about sneaking off to a corner to chat. For weeks now you've been pestering me with a million questions. Now when I'm ready to talk, the cat's got your tongue. Why is that?''

''Because it doesn't make sense. Neither does that comment about the love of a good woman. I think you're making fun of me, Slade Sutton.''

He set his plate down and cupped her face in his hands, hands that were just a little rough from hard work. Hands capable of incredible tenderness, she discovered.

''Maybe I'm just waking up,'' he said, his gaze

fixed on her mouth. "I'd like to kiss you, Val. You going to turn skittish if I do?"

Her breath caught in her throat. Finally, after all these months, he was going to kiss her. It was what she'd been praying for. She'd imagined his lips on hers a thousand times. She'd ached to have him wake up and notice her.

Because she couldn't have gotten a word past the lump in her throat if she'd tried, she simply shook her head.

Slade smiled. "Okay, then."

He lowered his head until there was little more than a sliver of air between his mouth and hers, and there he stopped. Anticipation shimmered through Val. It required all of her willpower to simply wait, when she wanted so desperately to close that distance and finally discover if he tasted half as wonderful as she'd imagined. Her heart pounded at the prospect. Her nerves rioted.

"Daddy!"

Annie's shrill, excited voice cut through the air. Slade jerked away so quickly, Val very nearly cried out at the loss.

"Hey, Daddy, look at me! I can dive off the board."

Slade glanced down into Val's eyes with mute apology. "Let's see, angel," he called out. He took Val's hand and urged her to come with him as he moved back toward the pool.

Sure enough, Annie executed a perfect dive off the low board. She swam to the edge of the pool and stared up at them hopefully.

"What did you think?"

"Awesome," Slade said. "How long have you been doing that?"

"Since a few minutes ago. Zack taught me."

"Then you're a natural," he praised. "Maybe we should see about getting you some diving lessons this summer, if it's something you'd like to do."

Her eyes shone. "Could I? Zack says there's a lady in town who gives lessons. She was in the Olympics once. She's really, really amazing. So, do you think we could call and find out if she'd take me?"

"First thing on Monday," he agreed. "Be sure you get her number from Zack."

She swam away happily to tell the twins what he'd agreed to.

"I can't believe she's that good," he said, staring after her, obviously awestruck.

"She has a real talent for it, that's for sure," Val agreed. "You handled that really well, you know."

Slade shrugged. "I just told her the truth."

"You did it instinctively. Seems to me you're getting your fatherhood legs back under you."

"I'll admit, I've been walking on eggshells since she got here. I guess for a minute there I forgot all the problems we've had and just reacted to her excitement."

"See how easy it is when you stop thinking so hard and worrying about every little thing?"

He gave her a rueful look. "Great advice, but if you ask me, it's easier said than done."

"Just keep trying," Val advised. "It'll get easier."

"I hope so," he said fervently.

"By the way, I'd be happy to drive her in for her lessons, if you can't get away. Laurie doesn't need me much these days, so I'm at loose ends."

Slade shook his head. "I can't ask you to do that."

"You didn't ask. I offered."

"Still, it's my responsibility."

"Which means it's up to you to make sure she gets there, right?"

He nodded cautiously, as if sensing a trap.

"And you've already found me to take her." She patted his arm. "Good job, Dad."

He frowned. "I think we ought to talk about me relying on you so much to help with Annie. It's not right."

"I'd much rather get back to that kiss that almost happened," Val countered.

He suddenly looked uncomfortable, as if she'd brought up a long-ago indiscretion that he regretted. "That was probably a mistake," he said.

"Why?"

To her irritation, he was acting as if she were trying to pin him down to set a wedding date. He wouldn't even meet her gaze.

"It just was, okay? Think of it as a momentary lapse in judgment."

She stared at him for a full minute and realized he was dead serious. He was dismissing all of that sizzling tension between them as if it had been no more than an unwanted fluke.

Furious, she lashed out. "Well, believe me, cowboy, it won't happen again."

She whirled around and walked away before he could see the humiliating tears that were stinging her eyes.

"Val."

She ignored the command in his voice and kept right on walking. She didn't stop until she'd reached the creek. Then she sat down in the shade of a tree and let the tears flow.

"Damned fool," she muttered, not certain whether she was thinking of herself or Slade when she said it. It probably didn't much matter. The label fit both of them just as neatly.

"Fool," Slade muttered under his breath as he watched Val storm off. He was forced to admit that she was justifiably furious.

He'd messed up good this time. He'd lost his head earlier, when he'd seen her in a skimpy little bathing suit barely covered by some sheer, floating material that purported to be some sort of robe. He'd reacted with a purely male surge of testosterone, rather than the caution that usually characterized his encounters with her. No wonder she'd been so baffled at first.

Oh, he'd been flirting all right. Walking straight down a very dangerous path. The only thing that had prevented him from making the mistake of a lifetime was Annie's interruption. He owed the kid diving lessons and a whole lot more for that. If only she'd been a little quicker, perhaps he could have avoided hurting Val's feelings, too.

"Where's Val?" Laurie asked, clearly undaunted by the scowl he shot at anyone who'd come close since Val's departure.

"Heading toward the creek last time I saw her," he said, trying not to squirm under her knowing gaze.

"Did you two have a fight?"

"What would your assistant and I have to fight about?"

"I can't imagine," she said lightly. "But it must have been something significant for her to run out on a party she pulled together for *your* daughter."

He glared at her, stung by the pointed reminder that he should be grateful to Val, rather than mistreating her. "Are you trying to make me feel even more guilty than I do?"

"Yes," she said without the least sign of contrition. "Val's a wonderful woman and you treat her abominably. If you're not interested, just tell her to back off."

"I have, on more than one occasion, as a matter of fact. She doesn't listen. Maybe you should recommend to her that she steer clear of me," he suggested.

"Believe me, I've tried. She seems to have the crazy idea that you need saving from yourself. She's also very fond of Annie. So am I, for that matter."

Relieved by the chance to change the subject, he seized the opening. "I hear you wrote a song for Annie."

Her expression brightened as it always did when she talked about her music. "As a matter of fact, I did. I was struggling with some lyrics and she said something that brought them into focus. I give her full credit."

"You going to sing it today?"

"Maybe." She gave him a look every bit as sly as

one of Harlan's. "If Val's around to hear it. I always like to get her reaction when I'm still fiddling with a new song."

"In other words, if I go find her and drag her back, you'll sing Annie's song."

"You're very quick for a cowboy."

"Whatever that means."

She patted his cheek. "For the record, I don't think you'll have to drag her back. Just be nice. Be honest. When you think about it, it's really not so terribly much to ask."

Slade put aside his plate of food for the second time that afternoon. At this rate, he wasn't even going to get a taste of the extravagant spread he'd paid for.

"Keep an eye on Annie for me," he said to Laurie.

"Not a problem."

He headed for the creek, debating all the way whether he had any business getting anywhere near Val. However, when he saw her sitting on a rock, shoulders slumped, staring despondently at the water, he knew he'd been right to come. He was the one who'd ruined the day for her.

He stopped several feet away. "I'm sorry," he said quietly.

She didn't look up, but her shoulders visibly stiffened. "For?"

"Starting something I shouldn't have. Saying what I did. Take your pick."

"How about for being a jerk?"

He grinned, accepting the judgment as fair. "That, too." He settled down on the huge boulder next to her.

"Why'd you do it?" she asked without turning her head.

"Which part?"

"Start something?"

"Because I took one look at you in that outfit and I wanted to be sure that no other man at the party started getting ideas." The words came out before he had a chance to censor them.

Her head swiveled toward him at that. Fire flashed in her eyes. "You were branding me?"

He winced at her indignant tone. "It wasn't like it was a conscious thing, but in a manner of speaking, yes, I suppose I was."

The answer clearly riled her. "If that is not the most egotistical, presumptuous thing I have ever heard in all my life."

"Guilty," he agreed. "I apologize again. I've got to say in my own defense, it took me by surprise, too, wanting you that badly."

She seemed startled by the admission and more than a little pleased. "You wanted me?"

"Oh, yeah," he said softly, his gaze traveling once more over the bathing suit that wasn't even partially concealed by that ridiculously flimsy cover-up.

"How about now?"

He struggled with the urge to show her, then finally resisted. He couldn't silence a heartfelt admission, though. "Oh, yeah," he murmured.

She nodded with satisfaction. "Good," she said, and stood up in a graceful, fluid move that practically had Slade's tongue hanging out. "I'm ready to go back now."

Great. He was so stirred up he was ready to throw her on the ground and make passionate love to her, and she was ready to return to the party.

All for the best, he told himself over and over as she sashayed past. Wasn't that exactly why he had come down here? Wasn't his only mission to get her back to the party? Hadn't he sworn not to get carried away again?

Oh, sure. Like it had never once crossed his mind on the way down here that he might just finish that kiss, after all. Liar, liar, liar! He was pathetic.

"Coming?" she inquired sweetly, amusement flashing in her eyes.

"You know, darlin', you're a little like TNT."

"Oh?"

"Small, but very volatile."

She gave a little nod of satisfaction, clearly pleased by the analogy. "Remember that the next time you get any crazy ideas about starting something you're not prepared to finish, cowboy."

"Oh, I'll remember it, believe me," he said fervently. In fact, he figured it would take a month of ice-cold showers to get this afternoon's little game out of his mind.

He managed to get through the rest of the afternoon without doing anything else crazy, but when evening came and the music began, he couldn't resist when Harlan Patrick all but shoved Val into his arms.

"Take over for me, pal. I'm going to find my wife," Harlan Patrick claimed. "Thanks for the dance, Val."

"Anytime," she said, her gaze fixed on Slade. "Well?"

Trapped, he held out a hand. "Would you care to dance?"

"Thank you," she said, moving into his arms as if she belonged there.

Holding her loosely, he stared down into her eyes. "You might want to reconsider this. Since my leg got banged up, I'm not so light on my feet."

Her gaze clung to his. "It's a slow song, Slade."

"So it is," he said, tightening his embrace until her head was tucked under his chin, her breasts pressed against his chest.

Big mistake, he concluded, when she was snuggled next to him. His blood heated to about one degree past boiling. Her rose-garden scent surrounded him, teasing at his senses.

It had been a long time since he'd held a woman this close, longer still since he'd wanted one with this aching neediness. Thank heaven she'd changed out of that provocative bathing suit. If he'd felt silky, bare skin beneath his touch, he'd have been lost.

Not that the sundress she wore was much of an improvement. Every time his hand slid up her back, his fingers brushed across soft, feminine flesh. And each time that happened, he could feel the shiver that washed over her. It was precisely the sort of responsiveness that made a man crave more. He was tempted to explore, to make the next caress more brazen and the one after that downright intimate.

He knew with everything in him that Val would be willing, even eager. A deeply ingrained sense of honor had him holding back. She was the kind of woman who deserved more than he had to give. She deserved pretty words and heartfelt whispers. She deserved happily ever after. He couldn't say for sure what tomorrow would bring, much less the day after that.

He realized with a start that she was staring at him, her expression troubled.

"Why so serious?" she asked.

"Counting the beats in the music," he lied. "If I don't, I'll stumble all over my feet and yours."

"Liar," she accused softly. "You were thinking too hard again, only this time it was about me, wasn't it?"

Her uncanny knack for reading his mind was disconcerting. "Maybe."

"I'll repeat what I said earlier. Sometimes it's smarter to go with your instincts."

He shook his head, wishing it were that simple. "A boy goes with his instincts, Val. A man—especially a man with a daughter to raise—has to stop to consider the consequences."

"So it was Annie on your mind just now?"

"No," he said firmly. "It was you. Only you."

"But you said—"

"I only meant that I can't just rush in and take what I want. It wouldn't be fair to you. It wouldn't be fair to Annie. I don't want her getting ideas about the two of us."

"That's very noble," Val said softly, but an increasingly familiar flash of fire in her eyes belied the quiet tone. "It's also bull."

He stumbled. "Excuse me. Did I hear you correctly?"

"You did. You're scared, Slade. That's what this is really about. You're terrified that if you let your guard down for one single second, you might actually have to deal with real emotions. You're terrified that whatever you start with me won't begin and end with sex."

He supposed there was a certain amount of truth in that. He'd let his emotions get the upper hand once and look where that had gotten him. Suzanne had ripped his heart in two.

"Maybe," he agreed, clearly surprising her.

"You're admitting it?"

"Sweetheart, I'm not oblivious to the truth. But saying it aloud doesn't change anything."

"Of course it does. Once you recognize the problem, you can start to move on."

He grinned at the simplicity of that. "Just like that, huh?"

"Exactly like that."

"You're forgetting one thing."

"What?"

"First, you have to want to move on."

She tripped. He steadied her, then met her gaze evenly. "I don't," he said succinctly.

"Well, of course you do," she said. "You can't want to go through life all alone."

"I'm not alone. I have Annie. I have my work. I have friends, including you, I hope."

"Friends? You and me?" She said it as incredulously as if he'd asked her to muck stalls with him.

"Why not?"

"Because…" she blustered, then stopped.

"Well?"

"Because it would never work."

"Why not? We're two intelligent adults. Surely we can keep our hands off each other, if we decide that's the sensible thing to do."

Her gaze locked with his. "What if I don't want to be sensible? What if I want to make a huge, glorious mistake by jumping into bed with you?"

"Then you'll be disappointed," he said firmly. "Because it isn't going to happen, Val. Not tonight. Not ever."

For some reason he couldn't fathom, she seemed to find his declaration amusing. "Is that so?"

"You can count on it."

"If you say so," she agreed mildly.

"We have an understanding then?" he asked, feeling it was somehow vital to get that nailed down.

"Oh, yes," she replied, with what could only be described as a silky purr.

Slade regarded her uneasily. She'd capitulated too easily. She'd said all the right things, all the things he wanted to hear. So why didn't he believe a word of it?

Maybe it was because even as she'd said the words, her gaze had been locked on his lips as if she'd never seen a more fascinating, more desirable mouth. Naturally that avid speculation had made him want to kiss her all over again.

Well, hell, he thought, as he took a decisive step back. This was going to be a whole lot harder than he'd anticipated. And Val, he predicted, wasn't going to do one single thing to make it any easier.

Chapter Seven

"The party was totally awesome," Annie declared as she walked home with her father afterward. She gazed up at him slyly. "I saw you dancing with Val. You were holding her real close. You like her, don't you?"

"She's a very nice woman," Slade said, hedging. This was exactly what he'd been afraid of—that Annie would start imagining a relationship where none existed.

Annie was having none of that. "Dad! You know what I mean. You really like her."

He scowled and put it more plainly. "Annie, don't go getting any ideas. Val and I are just friends, nothing more."

"I think she likes you," she added, as if he hadn't

spoken. "She gets this funny look on her face when she sees you, kinda like she's got a fever or something."

Slade wondered how Val would feel about *that* description. She'd probably welcome it, declare Annie to be a very bright, intuitive child. Which she was, of course, even if it was irksome.

"What makes you think this look she gets on her face has anything to do with me?" he asked, curious about a ten-year-old's reasoning when it came to romance. Maybe if he understood it, he could nip these crazy ideas in the bud.

Annie regarded him as if he were dense. "Because she only looks that way when she sees you, silly."

"And you think it's because she likes me? Why?" he persisted.

"Because it's the way Laurie looks at Harlan Patrick, and she loves him, right? So it must mean that Val at least likes you a little."

Ah, Slade thought, *that* look. Laurie and Harlan Patrick did stare at each other like a couple of lovesick calves most of the time. To Slade's surprise, not even marriage had wiped that expression off their faces. Maybe they were still in the honeymoon stage.

Come to think of it, though, most of the Adamses wore that look when they spotted their mates. Even Harlan and Janet, who'd been married for years, brightened when they saw each other. Slade hadn't thought such infatuation could last past the marriage vows, but in this family it had. He still thought it was probably an anomaly, something all but impossible for an outsider to obtain.

"Look, kiddo, I meant what I said. Don't go getting any ideas about me and Val, okay? I'm not looking to get married again."

"What about a mom, though? I could really use one," Annie declared in a wistful way guaranteed to snatch the rug out from under him.

"I'm sorry," he said sympathetically. "I'm afraid it's not in the cards. But I think Val would very much like to be your friend."

Annie sighed heavily. "It's not the same."

Slade sighed, too. "I know, darlin'." Even though he'd declared that to be his own goal earlier, having Val for a friend didn't seem likely to measure up for him, either.

"You look pleased with yourself," Laurie said, when she found Val sitting at the kitchen table with a cup of tea the next morning. "Basking in your success?"

"Which success would that be?"

"I was thinking of the party. What about you?"

Val gave her a grin. "I was thinking about the fact that I very nearly provoked Slade into forgetting all about those rigid principles of his. Of course, he dredged them up at the last second and spoiled things, but it was promising."

Laurie poured herself a cup of tea and sat down opposite her, her expression suddenly serious. "I thought principles were a rare thing in a man, so rare that they should be treasured when we stumble across them."

"They are," Val agreed. "Up to a point."

"In other words, the man still refuses to let you seduce him."

"So far," Val said, undaunted. "I think he's weakening, though."

"What happens if he does?" Laurie asked pointedly. "What happens if you finally succeed in getting him into bed, maybe just one time, and that's as far as it goes? Would you be satisfied with that?"

Val scowled. "No," she admitted. "I'm in this for the long haul."

"Then isn't it better that one of you is exercising some restraint?"

She considered Laurie's reasoning. "Okay, yes, but I really hate it when you're right," she grumbled.

Laurie chuckled. "I'm sure. Harlan Patrick complains about it, too."

Val reached for one of the homemade cinnamon buns that the housekeeper at White Pines had brought down still warm from the oven. It was scant consolation for reining in her longing to make some significant progress with Slade, but it would do. All that sugar was guaranteed to give her a rush.

"Do you have any real work for me to do today?" she asked Laurie hopefully. She desperately needed something to occupy her mind, to keep it off of Slade.

"Sorry, I can't help you," Laurie said without genuine regret. "We're on vacation, remember? If hanging around here is getting to you, you could always take a trip. Maybe some time away would help you to put things in perspective. Go on up to Nashville and go out with some of those men who are always hanging around when we're in town."

Val considered the idea and dismissed it. Being idle at White Pines with Slade nearby was still a vast improvement over anything else she could think of to do, even if she did spend every day all hot and bothered with no relief in sight. As for the men who'd pursued her over the years in Nashville, not a one fascinated her as Slade did.

"Maybe I'll just go and see what Annie's up to."

"I suspect you're going to have to find a playmate your own age now," Laurie teased. "Your party accomplished exactly what you set out for it to do. Annie's made new friends."

"Maybe I'll just round up a whole bunch of them and take them to a movie in Garden City," she said, recognizing that Laurie was probably right again.

"Or you could call Nick and see if he has work for you to do. You know my agent—he never takes a vacation."

"I'd rather go to a movie," Val said. Maybe, if she was very clever about how she went about it, she could get Slade to come along.

As she stood up to leave, Laurie shot her a knowing look. "I imagine you'll find Slade in the new corral working with that stallion he and Harlan Patrick just bought."

"I never said anything about going to look for Slade."

"Didn't have to," Laurie said. "You're very predictable. Have been ever since you laid eyes on him."

Val paused thoughtfully. "Maybe that's my problem. Maybe I'm too predictable."

"Oh, no," Laurie said, regarding her worriedly. "I

don't like that gleam in your eyes. What are you up to, Val?''

''Just coming up with a new plan,'' she said innocently. ''Nothing drastic. I won't embarrass you.''

Laurie waved off that concern. ''You couldn't embarrass me if you tried. I just don't want to see you get hurt.''

''Hey, no risk, no glory,'' she said blithely, and went in search of Annie.

Contrary to her original scheme, she did not try to manipulate things so that Slade would go along with her to chaperone a bunch of kids at the movies. In fact, she avoided him altogether, leaving it to Annie to get his permission for the outing.

When Annie mentioned that her diving lesson had been scheduled for the next day, Val volunteered to drive her. Afterward, they went out for the pizza Annie never tired of. Back at the ranch, Val dropped Annie off in front of her house, then drove on to Laurie's.

That was the pattern they fell into for the next couple of weeks. She rarely caught more than a glimpse of Slade. She gave him a casual wave and moved on, hoping that it was driving him to distraction the same way it was her.

At the end of the second week, after one of her diving lessons, Annie said, ''Dad wants me home for dinner tonight.'' She wrinkled her nose when she said it.

Val tried not to let her disappointment show. ''Oh? Does he have something special planned?''

''No. He says I'm taking advantage of you. He says

he is perfectly capable of feeding me,'' she said, probably quoting him verbatim.

Val barely resisted the urge to smile. "I'm sure he is.''

"That's what you think," Annie said with obvious disgust. "His idea of food is a frozen dinner he's nuked beyond recognition. He went shopping the other day and came home with five different versions of macaroni and cheese and six different versions of fried chicken and mashed potatoes. They all taste like burned rubber when he's done.''

It was hardly news that Slade couldn't cook. He'd admitted as much himself. Val just hadn't realized precisely how bad he was.

Fortunately, she could offer a solution. She loved to cook, though she rarely had an opportunity when Laurie was on the road and going from hotel to hotel. Even here Val never had a chance to spend time in the kitchen. Laurie enjoyed showing off her domestic skills for her new husband, and Val was always invited along. Even when she begged off, it was only to eat in town or have a sandwich in her room.

She considered the best way to handle this. She doubted Slade would respond to any hints she offered about teaching him to cook, but Annie was likely to be a more than willing student. She was clearly sick to death of frozen dinners.

"I could help out," she suggested carefully.

Annie's expression brightened. "Would you? I mean, Daddy would probably say no," she said, echoing Val's own assessment. "But maybe he wouldn't have to find out about it. Not at first, anyway."

"We can't lie to your father," Val objected, though probably not as strenuously as she should have.

"It wouldn't be lying. Not really," Annie insisted. "You could just come over in the afternoon and give me cooking lessons. By the time he gets home, dinner will be on the table. He won't know I didn't do it all myself."

"Honey, I think he'll suspect that something's going on. It's not like you can suddenly start fixing perfect pot roast overnight."

"I'll buy a cookbook and tell him I'm learning a new recipe every day. If you can read, you can cook, right? Once he tastes something that actually has real flavor to it, he won't complain," Annie said persuasively. "Please."

Val debated the wisdom of allowing Annie to deceive her father, of actually being a party to that deception. She weighed that against the old adage that the way to a man's heart was through his stomach.

"We'll try it tomorrow and see how it goes," she said finally. "If your father gets the least bit suspicious, you tell him the truth. You do not lie to him. Understood?"

Annie nodded eagerly. "Can we really do pot roast? Grandma made awesome pot roast. I really miss it."

"I'll pick up the ingredients in town in the morning. I'll meet you at your house at two. Okay?"

"Perfect. Daddy never gets home before five-thirty or six. Is that long enough?"

"Perfect," Val agreed. Whether he knew it or not,

Slade was about to be treated to the way his life could be if he'd just wake up and allow her into it.

Slade smelled the aroma of pot roast wafting from his house before he got within ten feet of it. His mouth watered. His suspicions kicked in, right along with a stirring of anticipation he didn't like one bit.

But when he walked inside, he found Annie at the stove lifting the lid on a huge pot. Half expecting to find Val, he was torn between disappointment and relief. She'd been avoiding him lately and he hadn't been nearly as grateful as he should have been. For a minute when he'd sniffed that pot roast, he'd been hoping that she was the one responsible. Maybe the housekeeper at White Pines had sent it down.

"What's that?" he asked, venturing close.

"Pot roast," Annie said proudly. "Doesn't it smell awesome?"

His gaze narrowed. "Who made it?"

"I did." She gestured toward a book that lay open on the counter. "It wasn't so hard. I just followed the directions."

He stepped up to the stove and peered into the pot. A roast indeed had been cooked to perfection. It was surrounded by carrots, onions and little potatoes, all perfectly done and seasoned with herbs.

"You did this?"

She nodded. "Are you hungry?"

"Starved," he admitted, deciding he'd pursue the issue of Annie's cooking after he'd had a chance to taste dinner. If it tasted half as good as it smelled, he doubted he'd have the heart to scold her.

"You wash up and I'll get it on the table," she said.

He noticed she had already set the small oak table with real dishes and place mats. She'd even plunked a vase of wildflowers in the middle. His little tomboy turning domestic? He wasn't buying it for a minute. Then again, maybe she was as sick of those frozen meals as he was. Maybe she'd been desperate for something edible. He wouldn't put it past her to take matters into her own hands. She was a lot like Val in that.

He took a quick shower, pulled on clean jeans and a T-shirt, then settled at the table. A steaming plate of food awaited him. Annie watched him expectantly. He cut a bite of the pot roast and tasted it. The meat almost melted in his mouth. It was even better than his mother's, and it was her specialty.

"Well?" Annie demanded eagerly. "How is it?"

"Better than Grandma's," he said candidly.

Her face lit up. "Really?"

"Taste it and see."

She took a bite, then beamed. "Oh, wow! I did it. I really did it."

After that, Slade didn't have the heart to question whether she'd done it entirely on her own. She was too darn pleased with herself. He told himself that was the only reason he let it pass.

The next night, when he found real southern fried chicken on the table, along with genuine mashed potatoes and gravy, he didn't want to spoil her obvious pleasure by getting into an argument.

He kept quiet the next night, too, when he found

homemade spaghetti waiting for him, accompanied by a zesty garlic bread and a fresh green salad.

When the desserts started turning up, he could no longer ignore his suspicions. He'd long since detected Val's hand in the increasingly elaborate meals, but his stomach had won out over his honor.

"The cake's real good, honey," he said as he savored the rich, moist chocolate with a frosting that might as well have been fudge, it was so thick.

"I know chocolate's your favorite. I told…" She stopped herself and a guilty flush climbed into her cheeks.

"Who'd you tell?" he demanded, seizing the opening.

"Val," she confessed in a whisper.

"Did she make the cake?"

"No," Annie said adamantly. "I did."

He leveled a gaze straight at her and waited.

"She just told me how,' she said finally.

"And the rest? Did she help with all of it?"

"She wanted to," Annie said with a defiant lift of her chin. "It was her idea."

"And whose idea was it not to tell me?"

"Mine."

"Why?"

"Because I figured you'd get mad. You said I was taking advantage of her, even though I knew it wasn't true. She likes to help."

Slade sighed. "I'm sure she does, Annie, but it's more complicated than that."

"How?"

"Val and I are just friends," he repeated for the

hundredth time. "It's not right to take advantage of a friend."

"But she said—"

"I don't care what she said," Slade said, his voice climbing. "This is going to stop."

"We'll starve to death," Annie muttered.

"We are not going to starve," he snapped in frustration. "There's nothing wrong with eating frozen dinners. Millions of people do."

"It's not the same as real food," Annie protested. "Especially after you've ruined it, anyway."

"Then we'll go into town to eat."

She jumped up then, practically quivering with outrage. "You do what you want. I'm going to live with Val."

She flew out the door before he could think to stop her. "Well, hell," he muttered, staring after her.

He waited a few minutes until his temper settled down, then went to look for her. He found her on the porch at Harlan Patrick's, sobbing in Val's arms. Val regarded him helplessly.

"What is this about?" she mouthed silently.

Slade sighed. "Dinner," he mouthed back.

Val's eyes filled with understanding. She stepped back and clasped Annie's shoulders, as she gazed into her eyes. "Why don't you take a walk down by the creek? I always feel better when I go there."

"What are you going to do?" she asked, not once glancing toward Slade.

"Your father and I are going to have a talk."

Annie turned toward him, then studied them both worriedly. "You're not going to fight, are you?"

"No," Slade said.

Val regarded him ruefully. "We might," she contradicted. "But we'll work it out, because that is what grown-ups do."

He supposed the comment was meant to effectively put him in his place. It succeeded.

He waited until after Annie had gone before he stepped onto the porch himself. He chose the swing and set it to swaying as Val moved into a rocking chair.

"I suppose I ought to start by thanking you for all the meals," he said stiffly.

She nodded. "That would be a good place to start."

"You shouldn't have, though."

"Why not?"

"Because—"

"Because you are too stiff-necked to accept help when it's offered?"

"Now wait a minute," he protested.

"Because you're scared I'm going to worm my way into your life?"

"Val—"

"Because you'd rather eat sawdust than something I enjoyed fixing for you?"

He moved quickly, scooping her out of the chair and clamping his mouth over hers before she could wind up and hit him with another accusation. The taste of her exploded inside him. The feel of her in his arms shattered the last of his restraint.

He gulped for air, then went back for more, sure that she was more potent than any female who'd ever crossed his path before. He'd never had a kiss shoot him straight to the moon. He'd never had the soft moan of a willing female fill him with such tenderness.

"Bad idea," he murmured, stepping away.

"No," she said, wrapping her arms around his neck and dragging him back.

With that single word, she dismissed all of his objections, all of his sound, rational thoughts and honorable intentions. With her mouth locked to his, he couldn't think at all, could barely even stand.

"Sweet heaven," he murmured, when she finally paused for breath.

"I can't believe I just did that," she whispered, her cheeks flaming. "I'm so sorry. I don't know what came over me. You've made it clear this wasn't what you wanted, and then you kissed me, and I guess I just went a little nuts. Sorry."

Smiling, he touched a finger to her lips. "Don't be. It was a long time coming. It was bound to happen."

"I thought you swore it would never happen."

"That was before you started chattering nonsense and I couldn't think of any other way to shut you up."

"It was effective, I'll give you that." She tilted her head and studied him. "What now?"

"Now we sit down and have a rational discussion about why it is all wrong for you to go on cooking for me."

She looked as if he'd slapped her. "No," she said. "That is precisely what we do not do. I will not have that conversation with you. Not tonight."

"Val—"

"I won't."

"We have to talk about it."

"Not tonight," she all but shouted.

"Okay," he soothed. "What do you want to talk about?"

A faint smile touched her lips. "I don't want to talk at all."

The subtly sensuous implications rocked him all over again. "Anything else is not an option," he said, his voice ragged. He took a few steps away from her. He grabbed the porch railing and stared out into the gathering darkness. "Did Annie tell you she intended to move in with you?"

"What?"

He heard the incredulous note in her voice and smiled. "She thinks she'll starve if I refuse to let you go on cooking for us."

"Could be she's right," Val said. "But I'll talk to her. I'm sure deep down she knows she can't live with me."

He felt her slip up to the railing beside him, standing just close enough to tantalize him with that flowery scent.

"Slade?"

"Yes."

"Other than your stubborn pride, why is it so wrong for me to help out?"

"It's not wrong," he said, raking his hand through his hair in a gesture of frustration. "It's just…" He couldn't come up with a better word.

"You're not taking advantage of me. Laurie's on

vacation. That means I have very little to do. I'm bored. I love to cook. It seems to me it works out well all the way around.''

She sounded so quietly reasonable, so sincere. He felt like a heel for robbing her of a chance to do something she enjoyed. "I'll pay you, then.''

"Don't insult me.''

He winced at the sharp tone. "Okay, then, I pay for the groceries, all of them, going back to when this started.''

"That's fair enough.''

"And you start sharing the meals with us.''

Her head snapped around at that. "Are you serious?''

"Yes,'' he said, smiling at her shock.

"Won't that make you crazy?''

"Yes,'' he said. "But not a minute passes that you don't make me crazy, so I might as well get the pleasure of a good meal and some adult conversation out of it.'' He tucked a finger under her chin and forced her to face him. "That's it, though. Food and conversation.''

A spark of amusement lit her eyes. "Food and conversation,'' she echoed dutifully.

And trouble, he thought to himself. Let's not forget about the trouble. He knew with every fiber of his being that he was asking for it.

Chapter Eight

"Haven't seen much of Val lately," Harlan Patrick said, the casual tone belied by the wicked glint in his eyes. "Any idea what she's been up to?"

Slade muttered a response he hoped would end the subject, though his boss wasn't known for taking a hint.

"What was that?" Harlan Patrick asked, his expression innocent.

Slade looked up and met his gaze evenly. "I said go to hell."

Harlan Patrick hooted, obviously undaunted by Slade's bad temper. "Now is that any way to treat your boss and the man who brought Val into your life?" he taunted.

"Probably no way to treat the boss," Slade agreed.

"As for the other, I probably ought to kick your butt from here to Dallas for inflicting that woman on me. From the minute you suggested I entertain her while you and Laurie dealt with your own family crisis, she's been pestering me to death."

"Which bothers you so much that you've started having dinner with her every night, just so you can keep an eye on her," Harlan Patrick teased. "Yep, you never know what a woman like Val might be up to. Gotta keep a close eye on her." He grinned. "Real close, I'd say."

"Like I said—"

"I know. I know. None of my business." Harlan Patrick's gaze turned serious. "Of course, Val and Laurie are more than business associates. They're friends. I'm right fond of Val myself. She helped me out when I was chasing after Laurie and trying to convince her to marry me. I'd feel real badly if anyone were to hurt her."

Slade regarded him evenly, accepting the fierce protectiveness that was typical of an Adams when one of their own was endangered. It extended to anyone they cared about. "Message received."

"Good," Harlan Patrick said with a sigh of relief. "Now I've done my duty. Maybe Laurie will get off my back."

Slade grinned. "So it was your wife who put you up to bugging me about this?"

"She's nesting," Harlan Patrick said. "I'm told it's natural with pregnant women. They want everyone around them settled down and happy."

Slade regarded him with surprise. "Laurie's pregnant?"

Harlan Patrick grinned, looking pleased as punch. "Yep. She found out yesterday, though Val told her she was weeks ago. I guess she recognized the signs from last time."

He said the last without rancor, though Slade knew for a fact it had been a very sore point that Laurie had kept his baby from him. If it hadn't been for a front-page picture in a tabloid, Harlan Patrick might never have known about his daughter, might never have made one last-ditch effort to get Laurie to marry him.

"Congratulations," Slade said, pumping his boss's hand. "I guess that means she won't be doing any concert tours for a while, then. That must make you happy." He also knew that Laurie's music and the traveling it required had been a real bone of contention between them before they'd married. The battles over it had been legendary until someone had finally taught the two the meaning of compromise. They were still struggling to get the knack of it, though, from what Slade had observed.

"Actually, the tour's still on," Harlan Patrick said with an air of resignation. "She claims she's healthy as a horse and there's no reason not to go ahead with her plans. I made her promise not to be on the road for at least two weeks before the baby's due. I'm not having my second child born in some other state with me nowhere to be found. I intend to be right by Laurie's side this time."

"You know, Harlan Patrick, sometimes Mother

Nature has a mind of her own,'' Slade pointed out. ''The baby might not stick to your timetable.''

''Which is why I'm going on the road with her for the last two weeks of the tour. I'm not taking any chances on missing this kid's arrival.'' He studied Slade. ''What about you? Were you there when Annie was born?''

Slade concentrated on cleaning Black Knight's shoe. ''Nope. I was on the circuit up in Wyoming then. Suzanne was back here in Texas. She never forgave me for it, either. My mama was at the hospital. She said Suzanne cursed me so loudly in the delivery room, it was a wonder I didn't hear it all the way up in Cheyenne.''

''I think we get the blame most of the time when women are in labor,'' Harlan Patrick said. ''I've been at the hospital on a few occasions waiting for various kids in this family to be born. Most of the men got cursed out to their faces. Ten minutes after they held the baby, though, it had all blown over.''

''Yeah, but with Suzanne and me, it was the beginning of the end. When I think back, it's probably a wonder our marriage lasted as long as it did after Annie came along. Suzanne was the kind of woman who required a lot of attention. I wasn't around to give it to her, and once Annie started school, they couldn't stay on the road with me.''

''That's a concern you'd never have with Val,'' Harlan Patrick noted, as if it were only an idle observation. ''Woman's as independent as they come.''

''So I've noticed,'' Slade said, and let it go at that. Val might claim to be interested in him, might even turn up at his table for dinner most nights, but she could vanish without a trace for hours on end. She didn't need him, not really. He was still struggling with himself over whether that was good or bad. Sometimes he found it more annoying than he cared to admit.

"Does that bother you?" Harlan Patrick asked, zeroing in on his thoughts as if able to read them.

"Of course not. She's entitled to a life of her own. It has nothing to do with me."

"Is that so?" Harlan Patrick inquired, his voice laced with skepticism. He grinned. "You are in such deep denial, it's pitiful."

Slade's head shot up. "Denial about what?"

"The way that woman gets to you."

"Don't go getting any ideas," he said, much as he did to Annie almost daily.

The trouble was, he was the one getting ideas. Some had to do with getting Val from the dinner table straight into his bed. Some had to do with the kind of permanence that scared him to death. Generally speaking, he figured it was better not to think about her at all. Unfortunately, ever since she'd taken over his kitchen, that had proved to be next to impossible.

Even on those occasions when she disappeared before he got home in the evening, her scent was everywhere. So was her touch. The table always had a bouquet of flowers on it. She and Annie had made curtains for the windows, sheer things that reminded him all too vividly of that provocative cover-up she'd worn at Annie's party. The magazines he'd tossed on the floor late at night sat in a neat little pile on a table.

A few weeks ago he might have accused her of trying to take over his life. Now he saw it as taking care of him…and Annie, of course. Instead of blind panic, a warm feeling settled over him as a result of her subtle improvements in his living conditions. The house suddenly felt a lot like a home, the kind he remembered from his childhood, not the kind he and Suzanne had shared on the rare occasions when he was there. The ever-present tension between him and his wife had robbed their home of any warmth or affection. Val made sure there was plenty of both. Sometimes her casual, innocent touches just about drove him to the brink.

The whole thing was worrisome, though. He was getting used to these feelings of being settled, getting used to *her*. Defenses rock-solid a few weeks ago were crumbling now. If he wasn't very, very careful he was going to forget all about his resolve to keep his distance—emotionally and physically.

With Harlan Patrick's warning still ringing in his ears, he reminded himself that that could be very risky in more ways than one.

Her plan to insinuate herself into Slade's life wasn't going the way she'd planned at all, Val concluded after several weeks of staring at him across the dinner table. They chatted politely. They laughed. They even exchanged long, heated looks once Annie left the table.

But when the dishes were done and Annie had retreated to her room, Slade all but escorted her out the door. He'd come close to slamming it in her face a couple of times. If he hadn't looked so panicked, she might have taken offense. Clearly the man didn't trust himself to be alone with her. His obvious skittishness, which was increasing almost daily, should have been reward enough, but she wanted more. A lot more.

Steering clear of Slade had worked the last time. Maybe it was time to return to that strategy. Sometimes even more drastic measures were called for. Maybe she needed to up the ante by bringing some competition into the mix. Slade had thrived on challenges once. He'd had a fiercely competitive career. She doubted that sort of spirit had faded just because he was no longer fighting for rodeo championships. Maybe he needed to be lured into fighting for her.

"Laurie, a lot of your songs are just about ready to go," she mentioned casually one morning as Laurie sipped some herbal tea to get her perpetually queasy stomach settled. "Why don't you get the band down here for a few days and rehearse? See how they sound with all the pieces in place?"

"Any particular reason you want the band to come?" Laurie shot her a knowing look. "You aren't, by any chance, thinking that a little attention from another man might make Slade jealous?"

"It could work," Val said defensively, not even trying to hide her motives from her best friend. "He doesn't have to know that none of the guys have ever looked at me twice."

"It's risky," Laurie warned, looking worried. "He might just conclude that you really have something going with one of the guys, that he was just a stand-in while you were stuck down here with me. If his pride kicks in, you'll be worse off than you are now.''

Val considered that, then decided it was still worth the risk. "I don't think I could be any worse off. Besides, I'm desperate to get him to wake up. Nothing else I've tried has worked."

"Ever heard of the word *patience?*"

"I've been patient," Val countered.

"Not by my standards, but okay." Laurie shrugged. "If it will stop you from moping around here, I'll do it," she agreed. "Call Nick and have him set it up."

Val grinned and reached for the phone. "I'll have them here by the weekend."

"Have you decided which of the men is going to be your secret admirer? I'm sure any one of them would be happy to volunteer. Contrary to what you believe, they have all looked at you twice. Sometimes more. None of them pursued it, because you made it very clear that you thought of them as business colleagues and nothing more." Laurie waved a finger under Val's nose. "See to it none of them get hurt. I've seen this kind of thing split up a band and I won't have it happening with mine, not because of some game you're bent on playing."

"I'll lay it all out up front," Val promised, chagrined by the understanding of what she was asking of Laurie, of the lengths her friend was willing to go to on her behalf.

When the band arrived on Friday, Val met them at the airport. On the drive to the ranch, she zeroed in on the drummer, who had a shy smile and sexy eyes.

She knew from past experience that men grew very competitive when he was around. He was also engaged to be married, which ought to make it safe enough to ask him to be part of her plot.

"Would you mind flirting outrageously with me for the next three or four days?" she asked him as the others unloaded their bags at the hotel. "Nothing serious. It's just to get someone's attention. I know it's a huge favor. I'll understand if you say no."

Paul studied her intently. "You know I'd do anything in the world for you, but you're going to have to clue me in. Are you trying to snag this man or run him off?"

"Snag him," she admitted.

He nodded, his expression serious. "Point him out and I'll get to work. But if you ever tell Tracy about this, I'm a dead man. She won't care that the flirting's not for real. She always thought I had a thing for you."

Val hesitated, remembering what Laurie had said about some of the band having been interested in her. "Maybe this is a bad idea, then. You and Tracy have something special. I don't want to start trouble."

"You won't," Paul assured her. "I know the score. This is nothing personal. Just don't kiss me like you mean it in front of the guys. They're the biggest blabbermouths I've ever run across." He winked. "Of course, if you want to kiss me in private, that's another story."

"If this goes the way I hope, I won't be kissing you at all," she said, then patted his cheek. "Don't look so disappointed. It's for the best."

At Val's instigation, Laurie invited Slade and Annie to the rehearsal on Saturday evening, along with
most of the Adamses. Annie dragged Slade over to
sit next to Val on the crowded sofa. They were
crushed together, thigh-to-thigh. Val could feel his
heat burning into her. Unless she was very much mistaken, his temperature had climbed several degrees
when he'd realized he couldn't squirm away from her
without causing a scene. To her amusement, he'd settled back stoically.

"I'm so excited," Annie confided. "Do you think
Laurie's going to sing the song I helped her write? I
know she did it at my party and all, but this is with
the whole band, like it would be on the album."

Val grinned. "I think you can count on it."

Slade's gaze locked with hers. "You haven't been
around much the last couple of days."

"Did you miss me?"

"Missed your cooking," he claimed, though the
look in his eyes said it was more than that.

"I've been busy helping Laurie set up this rehearsal. I wanted to spend some time with the guys,
too. You know, catching up." She allowed her gaze
to drift to Paul, who winked at her. She felt the heat
rise in her cheeks.

"Who is that?" Slade asked, his tone suddenly
testy.

"Paul McDaniels. He's been with Laurie from the
beginning. He's a great drummer. A nice man, too."

Paul came over then, standing close and resting his
hand on her shoulder in a familiar, possessive gesture.
Val introduced him to Slade and tried not to chuckle

at Slade's sour expression when Paul bent down to brush a kiss across her cheek before he went back to join the band.

"You two seem close," Slade said tightly.

"Old friends," she said simply, keeping her gaze on Paul as she said it. She managed to imbue her words with a significance that indicated the relationship went well beyond friendship.

"I see."

The tension radiating from Slade was almost palpable as the rehearsal got underway. He stared at Paul and scowled, as Laurie sang song after song. Only when the first strains of Annie's song filled the air did he manage to drag his attention away from the band to focus on Laurie.

"That's it, Daddy," Annie said, bouncing beside him. "That's my song. Listen."

He grinned at her enthusiasm. As Laurie sang about second chances and new self-discovery, his expression turned thoughtful. When the song ended, he leaned down and gave Annie a kiss.

"You should be real proud, angel. That was a beautiful song." He gazed at Val. "Thank you for giving her the chance to be a part of it."

He stood up then. "I think I'll be going now. I've got an early day tomorrow. Have to get to Fort Worth. Annie'll be staying with Dani and her kids while I'm gone. That should give you plenty of time to visit with your old friend."

Val barely managed to conceal her disappointment, then and over the next few days, during which Slade remained out of town. By the time he came back, the band had returned to Nashville.

As near as she could tell, her scheme had been a bust. For lack of anything more interesting to do, she saw no reason not to go back to the old pattern of cooking for Slade and Annie. For the next couple of weeks, she deliberately breezed in and out of their lives, leaving a trail of perfume and the aroma of freshly baked apple pie, Slade's favorite after her decadent chocolate cake.

However, somewhere along the way, she had concluded that tactical retreat was still her best bet. She made sure she was never there to share the meals she and Annie prepared. Maybe he'd actually miss her— eventually.

She was slipping out the door on a Friday night when Slade managed to catch her.

"Well, well, if it isn't the elusive homemaker," he said, amusement threading through his voice. "What are you up to?"

"Just seeing that the two of you don't starve to death, as usual." She ducked under his arm. "See ya. Gotta run."

He snagged her arm. "Oh, no, you don't."

"Slade," she began, but the protest died on her lips. The glint in his eyes was worrisome. "Slade?"

"You brought enough dinner for two?" he asked.

Because her lips were suddenly too dry for her to speak, she nodded.

"Then you'll have to stay and share. Annie's gone for the evening. A slumber party."

"Oh, really." Annie hadn't said a word to her

when she'd left the house a little earlier. She'd made some excuse about running up to the main house. She'd even begged Val to wait until she got back.

"You didn't know?" he asked, sounding genuinely surprised. "I thought you two were thick as thieves."

"I guess she forgot to mention it," Val said, recalling the evasiveness Annie had displayed earlier. The little schemer had set her up.

"So, will you stay?"

"Are you sure you want me to?"

"I suppose that depends on how dangerously you like to live." His gaze settled on her mouth, lingered, then rose to meet her eyes. "Or how involved you are with the drummer."

"I told you, Paul and I are friends."

"Good," he said succinctly. "That leaves us with deciding how much of a risk-taker you are."

"Risk-taker?" she echoed. She was cool, calm, dependable Val. She never took risks unless they were carefully calculated.

He nodded and lowered his head until his lips were almost touching hers. She held her breath and waited, almost certain she would die if he didn't close that infinitesimal gap Instead, he pulled back and grinned.

"Like I said, Val, it's time to decide just how dangerously you want to live."

She had a feeling he was toying with her, pushing her to admit that she had deliberately tried to make him jealous by flirting outrageously with Paul right in front of him. For all she knew, he'd asked Laurie, or even Paul, if there was really anything for him to be jealous about.

Impulsively, she reached up and threaded her fingers through his hair. "Paul who?"

She kissed Slade until she felt him tremble, then pulled away, forcing her expression into a deliberately nonchalant mask. "Still up for this, cowboy?"

As it turned out, Slade was very much up for it...and then some.

Chapter Nine

Carrying Val off to his bedroom struck Slade as being both the smartest and the dumbest thing he'd ever considered. She was the kind of woman any man would count himself lucky to have in his bed. He knew there was a sizzling passion between them just waiting to explode. He sensed she would be every bit as generous in bed as she was in other ways.

At the same time, he also knew that he wouldn't walk away from the experience unscathed. He'd already become addicted to setting off those sparks in her eyes, to seeing her mouth curve into a slow smile. What would happen when he'd experienced the most intimate caresses? When her body had welcomed him?

Worse, he was taking advantage of her, taking what

she offered without being willing to offer her anything in return except what they shared in bed. He
was setting himself up for guilt and her up for heart-
ache.

Knowing that, he actually managed to get himself
to halt at the door to his room.

"You can call it quits now," he said, his voice
husky. "No harm, no foul."

"Not a chance, cowboy."

The sparkle of anticipation in her eyes was as
bright as a star. Gazing into her eyes, he knew there
wasn't a chance in hell he could turn back now. He
wanted it all, needed her in ways he'd sworn never
to need a woman again. Sex was one thing. This was
something else entirely, no matter how hard he tried
to convince himself otherwise.

It was barely dusk outside and the room was in
shadows. Slade wanted it that way. As desperately as
he wanted to see every inch of Val, he was just as
desperate to keep her from getting a good look at the
scars from the accident. His leg wasn't a pretty picture. Suzanne had made it clear more than once that
the crisscrossing of stitches disgusted her. He had to
assume that most women would feel the same.

As Val's fingers lightly touched his cheek, his attention snapped back to the here and now, back to a
touch so tender it set off longing right along with
fireworks. He pushed all thoughts of his ex-wife from
his head and concentrated on the woman who could
make him weak-kneed with a glance.

He settled her on the edge of the bed, then sat next
to her. When she reached for the buttons on his shirt,

he stilled her hand. "Slowly, darlin'. We have all the time in the world."

She gave him a faint smile. "I keep thinking you'll change your mind. You have before. And dinner is on the table."

"Dinner can wait."

"It'll be ruined," she lamented.

"It can be heated up again. You seem to forget that I was used to ruined before you came along."

She touched a hand to his cheek once more. "So this is it then? You're not going to back out?"

"Not this time," he assured her. "Remember something. We've never gotten to this point before, and for good reason. I knew once we did, I'd never be able to stop." He smiled slowly. "Now let's get back to where we were before I brought you in here."

"You mean this?" Val asked, touching his lips with her own in a kiss so light he might have only imagined it.

"More like this," he said, taking her mouth with a hungry urgency that had them both quivering with need.

This time he was the one reaching for buttons, fumbling with them until her blouse was stripped away. Her bra—no more than a tantalizing scrap of lace— followed. His breath caught in his throat at the sight of her.

"You are…" Words failed him, as they often did when he was struck by her beauty.

"So are you," she teased, working her hands under his shirt and skimming nails over his chest, and then lower, until he had to swallow hard and slow their progress.

"Magnificent," she whispered, supplying the word that had eluded him.

He captured her attention with kisses that ventured from lips to neck to breasts and then, as he skimmed her slacks down, to far more intimate places. She gasped and writhed at his increasingly clever caresses.

"Not yet," she pleaded, when he clearly had her at the edge. "I…want…you…with…me." The words came out as a choked cry of need.

With the room in darkness now, Slade didn't hesitate. "I will be, darlin'," he promised, shucking his jeans and entering her just as she reached the peak and tumbled over.

She was still trembling in the aftermath of that first sweet climax, when he began to move inside her. He saw her eyes widen, then darken with pleasure as he rode her to the top again. He held back, counted to a hundred, blanked out everything in an effort to make the moment when they both shattered together even sweeter.

His body ached with the effort, but it was the kind of torment that men prayed for.

"Oh, Slade, don't," she begged, only to change her mind when he slowed. "No, please, more."

He lifted her hips off the bed and drove into her, one last, deep plunge that ripped a moan from low in her throat and had him screaming out her name as skyrockets went off inside him.

It was a long time before he could catch his breath, longer still before he could think of what to say.

"Sweet heaven, I think you've destroyed me," he murmured, pressing a kiss to her brow, then collapsing back against the pillows.

She gave him a smile of purely feminine satisfaction. "Is that so?"

"You seem pleased about it."

"If it means you won't soon forget about me, I am."

"Darlin', I couldn't forget about you if I tried. I know that from experience," he said ruefully. If it had been difficult before, it was going to be downright impossible now that he knew the wonder of being with her like this.

Maybe he didn't have to forget about her. Maybe there was an answer that would work for both of them. As Val lay curled contentedly against him, he began to toy with a notion that he had dismissed on more than one occasion before tonight.

Tonight had changed things. There was no going back. Maybe his solution would take them forward. Now all he had to do was work up the courage to bring it up and hope for the right words to explain it.

In the meantime, he was stunned to discover that he wanted her again, that once hadn't been nearly enough. He reached for her, only to have her slip beyond his touch and flip on the light.

"No," he said harshly, shoving past her to turn it off again.

She stilled as if he'd slapped her. "Slade?" Her voice was filled with questions. There was no mistaking the fact that his reaction had hurt her.

"Sorry. There's no need for light."

"Why? What are you afraid of?"

"Who says I'm afraid?"

"You must be. I know you like looking at me. I could see it in your eyes before. Why won't you let me see you?"

He lay back against the pillow, silently cursing her quick mind and his own scars.

"I'm not going to let it rest until you tell me, so you might as well stop stalling," she said, as briskly as she might have handled some business associate who wasn't fulfilling a promise.

Slade drew in a deep breath. Better to admit the truth and gauge her reaction, especially if he intended to go through with his impulsive plan. He couldn't spend the rest of his life hiding in the dark, not around a woman like Val. She'd never allow it.

"There are scars," he said finally.

"From the accident?"

He nodded, then realized she couldn't see. "Yes," he said more curtly than he'd intended.

"You never talk about what happened."

"Why talk about it? It's over with."

"Tell me anyway. Annie says it was your wife's fault and that it robbed you of your career."

His daughter's insight stunned him. "She knows all that?"

"She says that's why you don't like her much, because she reminds you of her mother."

He muttered a harsh expletive. "I had no idea she thought that."

"Is it true? Does she remind you of her mother?"

"She looks like her, that's true enough, but that's

where it ends. Annie's always been my treasure. From the first moment I laid eyes on her, I was in awe that I could have created something so beautiful.'' He sighed. ''I guess somewhere in the past year or so, I stopped reminding her of that.''

''She needs to hear it,'' Val said gently.

''Yes,'' he agreed.

When he fell silent and stayed that way, Val prompted, ''You were going to tell me about the accident.''

He smiled ruefully in the darkness. ''Was I now?''

''Oh, yes,'' she insisted.

''I was back in Wilder's Glen to see Suzanne and Annie. Suzanne hated it there. It was too small-town for her. She missed being on the road with me, but Annie needed to be settled. She needed to be in school. I didn't know it at the time, but Suzanne took every opportunity to dump Annie with my parents so she could go chasing around, having the same kind of fun she assumed I was having on the road and denying her.''

He expected some reaction, but Val remained absolutely silent. Instead, she simply reached for his hand and linked her fingers with his. Oddly, the gesture brought him a measure of peace he rarely felt when he thought back to that tumultuous time.

''Suzanne wanted to go out,'' he said, recalling the argument they'd had about it. ''I'd barely walked in the door. I wanted to stay at home, spend some time with my daughter and my wife in private. Still, I could see her point. I thought she'd been trapped at home while I was away, and deserved a break from it. We went out for dinner, even danced a little, though I was aching from the last rodeo.''

He grimaced at the understatement. He'd grown used to aches and pains over the years, but it had been worse that night. He'd lost his concentration in the ring and been tossed off the back of a bull. It had been a miracle he hadn't been trampled.

"We finally left the bar after midnight. I was so exhausted, Suzanne volunteered to drive. She wasn't drunk. Hadn't even had a beer, for that matter. On the way home, she started in on me again about being left behind all the time, about being stuck in Wilder's Glen where my parents could watch her every move. We argued.''

He could still hear her voice echoing in his head. "It was the same old thing, a fight we'd had a million times before, but she was driving too fast, paying too little attention to the road. There was a sharp curve and she missed it. We slammed head-on into a tree.''

Val gasped softly.

Slade kept his voice dispassionate, even though he could still hear the grinding of the metal, feel the searing pain. "The damage was mostly on the passenger side. My leg was crushed. For a while the doctors thought I'd lose it, but I fought them every step of the way. Eventually it healed, just not well enough for me to go back to the rodeo. Being married to a rodeo star had been enough for Suzanne, enough to compensate for being left behind to raise our daughter. Without that, with me scarred, she saw no reason to stay. As soon as the verdict was in on my future, she took off. She filed for divorce a week later. She didn't even fight me for custody of Annie. She seemed almost glad to be rid of her.''

''What a horrible person,'' Val said indignantly. ''I thought for better or for worse was supposed to mean something.''

She moved swiftly, too swiftly for him to stop her. Before he could guess her intentions, her hand was on his damaged leg.

''No,'' he said curtly, trying to grab her hand.

She shook him off, then began to trace his scars with a touch so gentle it took his breath away. His injuries had healed long ago, but not his soul. Val's touch did that. When her lips brushed over each and every ridge of scar tissue, the protective shield around his heart shattered.

He knew in that instant that his earlier decision had been a sound one. She was the one woman in the world with whom he could build a future.

''That was a long time coming,'' Slade noted when they finally got around to dinner sometime in the middle of the night. Even reheated, the food was a whole lot better than anything he'd ever fixed.

''Are you referring to our meal?'' Val inquired.

He held back the desire to grin at her testy tone. ''You know I'm not.''

She put down her fork and met his gaze evenly. ''What now, Slade? Are we going to talk about what's next?''

Leave it to Val to be direct. He decided to see what she was thinking before laying out his own ideas. ''You tell me. You seem to be the planner in the room.'' He watched her struggle with that for a minute, but Val wasn't easily caught off guard.

"I say we give it six months and see how it goes," she said briskly. "That ought to tell us if this is some sort of a fluke."

The response irked him. He'd mentally moved way past a trial run. "Oh, really?" he said irritably. "Six months? And how do we explain our relationship to my daughter during that time? Or do we sneak around the way her mama did? That would certainly keep the excitement alive."

"I was under the impression that you didn't bother to explain much to Annie," Val said, matching his sarcasm.

He put a hand to his chest. "*Wham!* A direct hit."

She winced guiltily, then sighed. "Okay, I was being glib. And unfair. You're right that Annie is at an impressionable age. We can't carry on right under her nose and get her hopes up. Any suggestions?"

This was it, Slade thought. The opening he'd been waiting for. He'd made his decision. It was time to put all his cards on the table.

"She adores you. You and I get along okay." He watched her expression closely, then added, "Why not just go for broke and get married?"

Val looked momentarily taken aback, but she recovered quickly. There was very strong evidence from the clatter of her silverware hitting her plate that the fire in her eyes was not sparked by passion.

"Now there's a proposal that will make a girl's heart go pitter-pat," she said with cool disdain.

Slade promptly took offense. He'd asked her to

marry him, hadn't he? "If you were expecting hearts and flowers, you picked the wrong guy. I don't believe in romance or love or happily ever after. I thought you knew that."

"Then what are we talking about here?" she demanded with rising indignation. "A mother for Annie? You'll make the ultimate sacrifice to see to it she has a real home?"

He squirmed uncomfortably. "More or less."

"And now that you've tested the sex and discovered it's terrific, that's just a bonus for you?"

This wasn't going well. He didn't have to be hit upside the head with an iron skillet to get that. The idea had popped into his mind weeks ago, sometime between the instant he'd first caught a whiff of her apple pie and the time all-too-recently when he'd lost himself inside her. The latter probably hadn't been the best time to reach any life-altering decisions.

"Maybe we should think about it some more," he suggested.

Val stood up and tossed her napkin in his face. "No need for that, cowboy. I'll marry you when hell freezes over."

Naturally, the second she flounced out the door, Slade realized that he'd actually done the one thing he'd never expected. He'd gone and fallen in love with the woman.

Watching her walk out on him left him with a sick feeling in the pit of his stomach.

"Well, that went well," he muttered. If it had gone any better, she'd probably be quitting her job and moving back to Nashville first thing in the morning.

"I think I'll take that vacation you suggested," Val said to Laurie in the morning. On the walk back from Slade's, she'd cursed a blue streak in the night air, then reached a decision. It was time to get away from temptation.

Her friend's gaze shot up. "Vacation? Why? I thought things were going better with Slade."

"Not so that you'd notice," she said, reluctant to admit just how far things had gone the night before, and even more reluctant to explain how they'd ended.

Laurie studied her intently and seemed to come to her own conclusions. "Well, you can't leave now," she said emphatically. "The recording sessions start in less than a month. We have to start kicking things into high gear. I need you."

"I can do the work in Nashville, then. It'll be even better. Nick and I can be in closer contact."

"You're my assistant, not Nick's," Laurie said firmly. "And I need you here." Her gaze narrowed. "As your friend, though, I'm asking if that's going to be a problem."

"No," Val said with a sigh. Her job was too important to her to give it up because she had made a huge mistake falling in love with Slade. "I'll make it work."

"For what it's worth, I'm sorry you're having a rough time. I could get Harlan Patrick to beat Slade up for you."

Val grinned despite herself. "No, but thanks."

"The offer's good anytime, if you change your mind."

"I won't," Val assured her. "Now what do you

need me to do today? Should I start finalizing the media plan?''

"That can wait," Laurie said. "Nick's supposed to send down the final schedule today or tomorrow. When we have it, you can start lining up interviews. We'll do radio shows in every city, so they'll push the tickets."

"Pushing tickets is not an issue," Val said. "You're already sold out in every city Nick has booked."

"Oh," Laurie said, looking genuinely surprised.

She still underestimated her own popularity. It was one of her charms, Val thought. She doubted Laurie would ever think of herself as the superstar she was. It wasn't in her nature to get a swelled head or to pull any prima donna stunts.

"I'll do the interviews anyway," she said, proving exactly what Val had been thinking. "I owe those guys for the airtime my songs get."

"I'll take care of it," Val promised.

"In the meantime, why don't you go for a walk? Or drive over to Garden City and go shopping?" She gave Val a sly look. "A new pair of sexy heels might make you feel better."

Val stuck her foot out and stared at it despondently. "See? Boots. You've turned me into a cowgirl."

"I know. That's why I suggested the heels. They might remind you of who you are."

Val wasn't sure if that was good or bad, but for lack of anything better to do, she nodded in agreement. "A shopping trip sounds good. Want to come?"

Laurie shook her head. "I have everything I need."

"Not baby clothes," she said. "Or wallpaper for the new nursery."

"The old nursery is just fine," Laurie said, but she was clearly tempted. "Harlan Patrick pulled out all the stops when he built it."

"But that's Amy Lynn's room. You know you're going to want something new for the baby. You'll be on the road the final months of your pregnancy. You won't have time to do this then."

"I could just leave it to my husband. He did okay last time."

"But you want a say in it," Val teased. "You know you do."

Laurie held up her hands in a gesture of surrender. "Okay, okay, let's do it. I'll get my charge cards and warn Harlan Patrick that I'm going on a spending spree."

"He'll probably suggest we fly to Dallas and invade Neiman-Marcus," Val said, more than a little intrigued by that idea herself.

"Why not?" Laurie said, getting into the spirit of it. "I'll tell him he can come along, if he'll fly us over. Give me an hour to persuade him."

Val chuckled at her determined expression. "An hour, huh? You must be good."

"I am," Laurie said with pride.

In fact, it took her little more than a half hour to find her husband and talk him into playing hooky for the day to go shopping for baby things.

"It's a good thing Granddaddy doesn't know where we're going or he'd insist on coming along," he said as they boarded his uncle's company jet. "Nothing he likes better than stocking a new nursery."

A few minutes later, he glanced back from the cockpit. "You guys all set back there?"

"Ready to go, Captain," Laurie said. She glanced over at Val. "Are you okay with this? It's not exactly a girls' day out with Harlan Patrick along."

"Having your husband along is fine with me, but he is probably the only man I could tolerate right now. As a gender, I've pretty much concluded they're dense as granite."

"As a gender?" Laurie teased. "Or just one particular man?"

"Okay, Slade. There, I've said his name. I don't want to hear it again for the rest of the day." She thought about it for a second, then added fervently, "Maybe even for the rest of my life."

Beside her, Laurie chuckled.

Val glared. "It is not a laughing matter."

"Oh, but it is," Laurie said. "I seem to remember someone all but laughing her head off when Harlan Patrick was giving me fits. Turnabout's fair play."

"Is this what I did to you?" Val asked.

"Pretty much."

"How annoying."

"It was," Laurie agreed. "But I forgave you, because I knew your heart was in the right place. Harlan Patrick and I belonged together."

"Yes, well, Slade and I don't."

"If you say so."

"I do," she said firmly. Maybe if she said it often enough, she'd finally start to believe it.

Chapter Ten

"So, how'd it go with Val last night?" Annie inquired when she caught up with Slade at midday.

He scowled. "None of your business."

For most of the morning, he'd been dreading Annie's return and the likelihood she'd be asking a question just like this one. He knew he'd gone about things all wrong, but he hadn't anticipated Val's violent reaction. After the way she'd chased him for months, after the way she'd taken Annie under her wing, he'd foolishly been convinced that she'd jump at the opportunity to marry him and become a mom to Annie. Her fiercely negative response just proved how little he knew about women.

Annie's expression fell at his blunt words. "Oh, no, Daddy. What did you do?"

"Who says I did anything?" he asked defensively. "Shouldn't you still be sound asleep at the slumber party or something?"

"Nobody sleeps at a slumber party," she pointed out. "That would ruin it."

Yet another example of the illogic of the female mind, he supposed. "Why don't you go on up to the house and read?" he suggested, grasping at straws to get some peace and quiet and avoid his daughter's judgmental gaze. "You got a whole armful of books from the library the other day."

"I was bored the other day. Now I'm not. I'll read them later." She faced him with a defiant tilt to her chin and her hands jammed into her pockets. "I thought maybe I could help you today."

He was in no mood to have her hanging around pestering him, asking more questions about Val that he didn't want to answer. Besides that, he couldn't imagine what a ten-year-old girl could do to help. She knew nothing about ranch work and next to nothing about horses. She was so skinny, she looked as if a stiff wind could blow her away.

"Not today," he said in a clipped tone. "Aren't some of the other kids around here someplace?"

He could read the hurt in her expression, but she squared her shoulders as if the dismissal didn't bother her in the least. He could practically see the pride kicking in.

"Never mind," she said stiffly. "You don't need to worry about me. I'll find something to do."

He watched her walk away, saw her shoulders slump dejectedly, and felt like kicking himself. What kind of rotten louse took out his frustrations on a little girl who was only trying to help? For an instant he was tempted to call her back, but it didn't take much to convince himself that she was better off finding one of the Adams kids to play with. Sticking around him in his present mood sure wouldn't be a lot of laughs. He was sick of his own company.

An hour later he was putting Black Knight through his paces when Hardy Jones came down to the paddock and propped his elbows on the rail. He watched the workout for a minute, then said, "As soon as you can take a break with that, I think you'd better come with me."

The usually jovial hand's grim tone set off alarms. "What's happened?" Slade demanded. "Is it Annie? Is she hurt? Or Val? Has something happened to Val?"

"No, no, they're both fine," Hardy said soothingly. "Sorry. I should have said that straight out. But there is a problem and it does involve Annie."

Only then did Slade notice the spark of amusement in the younger man's eyes that he was struggling unsuccessfully to hide. It was a look that went with mischief, not calamity.

"Oh, no," Slade muttered. "I'm really going to hate this, aren't I?"

"More than likely," Hardy agreed cheerfully. "Just remember, it's not the end of the world. From what I've heard since I started working here, there have been worse stunts over the years. Our boss and Justin were behind a few of them. Harlan Patrick survived to take charge, and Justin turned into a straight-arrow. I'm sure Annie will outlive this as well.''

Being reminded of Harlan Patrick's and Justin's legendary exploits was not at all reassuring. ''Maybe you'd better just tell me. That way I'll be prepared for the shock.''

''Not a chance,'' Hardy said. ''Why should I ruin the opportunity to see your face when you find out what Annie's been up to.''

Slade scowled. ''You are a diabolical man. One of these days one of those ladies you like to flirt with is going to snag you, but good. Personally, I can't wait to see it.''

The notorious womanizer merely grinned. ''Never happen,'' he said with the total confidence of a man destined to take a serious fall.

A tight knot formed in Slade's belly as they headed up the road toward his house. What the devil had Annie done? Had she burned the place down? He sniffed the air, fully expecting to smell smoke. To his relief, none was discernible.

As they rounded a curve in the road and his house appeared, his mouth gaped.

''What the dickens has she done?'' he murmured, staring at the fresh coat of bright pink paint that decorated the lower half of the house and most of Annie. She was sitting on the front steps, arms folded protectively across her middle, a stubborn jut to her chin.

''Quite a picture, isn't it?'' Hardy inquired, laughter lacing his voice.

''Where in God's name did she find paint that color?''

"Mixed it herself, from what I hear. There was a can of white paint and a can of red in the storage shed. I give her credit for ingenuity. Of course, it was indoor paint, but she didn't know the difference."

"I'll call Harlan and Cody right away, make sure they know not to worry," Slade said, his expression grim. "I'll have the house painted white again by tomorrow."

"I'm not worried," Harlan assured him, picking that precise moment to pay a call. Obviously the news of Annie's adventure had traveled fast. His eyes glittered with amusement. "You should have seen the multihued shed Jenny created in an act of pure rebellion years back. This is downright sedate by comparison."

"I don't suppose you related that story to Annie," Slade said, beginning to understand where Annie might have gotten the idea to do something so outrageous.

"I suppose it could have come up," Harlan admitted without the slightest hint of guilt. "I enjoy telling tales about my family."

Slade got the distinct impression he found the stories highly entertaining in retrospect. Slade wondered if the rancher had taken them in the same spirit when they happened. Probably so. That was the kind of man Harlan Adams was—tolerant to a fault.

"Are you sure you don't pass along these stories just to put ideas into the heads of your great-grandchildren?" he asked the old man. "Is that your way of getting even for what your children and grandchildren did years ago?"

"It might have crossed my mind that they deserved a little payback for past misdeeds," he admitted unrepentantly.

"I can't decide which of you to strangle first," Slade muttered. "Though I suppose you're pretty much off-limits."

"Pretty much," Harlan agreed. "And my sympathy is with Annie. After all, the girl was just indulging in a little self-expression. In fact, if she hadn't run out of paint, I might have helped her finish the job."

"Thank goodness for small favors," Slade said fervently. He glanced at Hardy, who was observing the exchange with evident fascination. "Thanks for bringing this to my attention. I'll take it from here."

Still grinning, Hardy took off for the bunkhouse. Harlan seemed less inclined to go.

"Don't you be too hard on the girl," he warned.

"Believe me, she'll get no more than she deserves," Slade said tersely.

After Harlan had gone, Slade strode up to the porch and scowled down at his daughter. "Mind explaining what the hell you were thinking of?" he all but shouted.

Annie's eyes blinked wide. "Daddy, you cussed."

"This isn't about my language," he said. "It's about this." He waved his hand in a gesture that encompassed the half-painted house. "Why, Annie?"

Her eyes blazed with self-righteous anger. "Because I needed something to do and I thought it would look pretty."

"I thought you hated pink," he said, as bemused by the color choice as by the painting itself.

"It's a girl color," she said, as if that explained it. Slade was mystified. "So?"

"I've tried and tried to do stuff you like," she said with evident frustration. "But you won't let me, so I figured maybe if I did girl stuff, you'd like me better."

She sounded so utterly sincere, so lost and lonely, that it came close to breaking his heart.

"Oh, Annie," Slade whispered, and sank down on the step beside her. When he opened his arms, she scrambled into them.

"I'm sorry, Daddy," she whispered. "I thought it would be pretty, but it's not." Her voice caught on a sob. "It's awful. And then Hardy came along and saw it and he started laughing."

Slade was surprised to find that he was chuckling himself. "I imagine he did."

She pulled away. "You're laughing, too. Does that mean you're not mad at me?"

"Oh, yes, I am mad at you," he corrected. "But as someone pointed out to me very recently, it's not the end of the world. We'll buy some white paint and fix it up in our spare time."

"You'll help?" she asked. "Even though I'm the one who made the mess?"

"I'll help. But you're going to do your share, young lady. And you're going to be grounded for a week. You will not leave the house while I'm at work. That'll give you a chance to do some thinking."

"Can I watch TV?"

Slade thought of the soap operas and talk shows that made up a huge percentage of daytime TV.

"Nope. You can read those library books." He caught a hint of something in her face and realized she was already reaching the same conclusion that he was—that no one would be around to see to it that she abided by the rules.

"Forget it," he said.

"Forget what?" she asked innocently.

"You can't sneak behind my back. I'll know."

"How?"

"Fatherly instinct."

"Do you really have that?" Annie asked skeptically.

Her response was more on target than Slade would have liked. "Okay, I'll get someone to stay here with you. That's how I'll know."

"Who?" she scoffed. "I'm too big for a babysitter."

He thought of Val and wondered if she was too furious with him to be called on in an emergency.

Annie's eyes glinted knowingly. "What about Val?"

"We'll see," he said.

"I could go over to Laurie's, so I wouldn't be any trouble," she suggested.

Slade shook his head. "No way. That would be too much like a treat. This is supposed to be punishment. Don't worry about it. I'll work it out."

"Okay, Daddy," she said meekly.

A little too meekly, Slade thought, casting a suspicious look at his daughter. Was it possible that this was exactly the outcome she'd been counting on? Was she that determined to see that something happened between him and Val? More than likely, he realized. Caught between two clever, sneaky females, a man didn't stand a chance.

After he'd finished work for the day, showered and changed, Slade turned up at Val's, hat in hand, at least figuratively speaking. Her greeting couldn't exactly be described as warm.

"Yes?" she said, not even stepping aside to let him in. She acted as if he were a peddler coming to sell vacuums.

"Could we talk for a minute?" he asked. Seeing Harlan Patrick and Laurie in the background, their expressions fascinated, he added, "Outside?"

"We're having dinner."

"I'll wait."

"I don't think so. I'm tired. I've been shopping in Dallas all day with Laurie."

"It won't take long."

Val sighed heavily. "Fine. Let's get it over with." She stepped outside and closed the door firmly behind her.

"This won't take a minute," Slade promised again, fighting the desire to sweep her into his arms and kiss her until that stern, unapproachable set to her lips disappeared.

"Maybe you should sit down," he suggested.

"You said it wouldn't take long."

Oh, she was still furious with him, all right. She had no intention of making this easy. And why should she? He'd insulted her. That was plain enough. He began to pace, trying to find the words to convince her to help him out of the jam in which he'd found himself.

"Okay, it's about Annie," he said finally. "I know I have no right to ask this, but I need someone to stay with her for a few days."

"Oh?"

"I suppose you heard what she did?"

Her expression softened and something that might have been the beginnings of a smile tugged at the corners of her mouth. "Oh, yes. It was the first thing we saw when we got back from our trip. It certainly is a cheerful color. It doesn't suit you at all."

Slade let the deliberate jab pass. "Well, I can't let her get away with it, of course. I've grounded her for a week, but I can't very well stop working to stay with her and see that she abides by the rules."

Val stiffened as if she'd already guessed what was coming next. "No."

"I haven't even asked yet."

"I'm not going to stay with her. She's your daughter, Slade, not mine. Hire a baby-sitter."

"She'd run roughshod over a babysitter. She needs someone she respects to keep her in line."

"And that's me?"

"You know it is. Look, if I could think of some other way, believe me, I'd grab it. I know how you feel about the two of us."

She gave him a penetrating look. "Do you really?"

"Yes. I suppose you like Annie well enough, but you're fit to be tied with me. Rightfully so, from your perspective."

"And from yours?"

"Okay, I have to admit, I don't entirely get it," he said. "I know you have feelings for me and, like I just said, you care about Annie. Was it so wrong to suggest we get married?"

"Yes," she said succinctly. "But I am not going to discuss it with a man as dense as you apparently are. It would be a waste of my breath."

"Try me."

She almost did. He could see that she was tempted to try to spell it all out for him, but at the last second, she apparently changed her mind. "I'll look out for Annie the next few days, but let's be clear on one thing. I am doing it for her sake, not yours."

Slade concluded now was not the time to press her about the rest. And at the moment, he was willing to accept her help on whatever terms she set. "Thank you."

"Don't thank me. Spending time with Annie is my pleasure. I wish you felt the same way."

Before he could respond to that, she'd whirled away and gone back inside, slamming the door in his face.

If Laurie and Harlan Patrick hadn't been right inside, he would have gone after her and kissed her silly, he told himself. As it was, he just sighed and wondered if he could manage to dig the hole he was in any deeper.

"How come things didn't go so good with you and Daddy the other night?" Annie asked within five minutes of Val's arrival the next morning.

Val noticed that Slade had already made himself

scarce. She told herself that was for the best, but deep down she knew she'd been hoping to catch at least a glimpse of him. Dumb, dumb, dumb! Hadn't she learned anything the past few days?

"So," Annie persisted. "What happened?"

"Who says anything happened?" she asked.

Annie gave her a pitying look. "I can tell. He's been mean as a snake and you haven't been around."

"Well, it's between your father and me."

Annie shook her head. "No, it's not. I live here, too, remember? I'm just a kid. Somebody ought to fill me in so I don't feel left out. Did you know that scars from childhood can last an entire lifetime?"

Val held back a grin. "Is that so? Where did you hear that?"

"On *Oprah.*"

"I thought you weren't supposed to be watching TV."

"Oh, this was a long time ago," Annie assured her. "Weeks and weeks ago at least. It was probably while I was still at Grandma's."

Val thought she was protesting a little too vehemently, but let it pass. "Well, right now, you are a kid who's in very big trouble. Let's concentrate on that instead of whatever deep psychological scars you think you might get from being left out of the loop."

Annie shrugged. "Whatever."

"Suppose you tell me what possessed you to paint the house."

"It seemed like a good idea at the time. Besides, it worked, didn't it?"

Val studied Annie intently. "Meaning?"

Annie suddenly seemed just a little too fascinated with her cereal. Val doubted she was counting the little os still floating in her bowl.

"Okay, kiddo, what are you up to?"

"Nothing, I swear it," Annie said, her expression totally innocent.

"I don't believe that for a minute."

"It's true. I just thought the house was a boring color, that's all." She wrinkled her nose. "Daddy wants to paint it back to white."

"And you don't?"

"Nope. I was thinking maybe yellow," she said, her gaze on Val, her expression serious. "What do you think? It's your favorite color, isn't it?"

"Yes," Val agreed. "I do like yellow, not that that should have anything to do with what color you decide to paint your house."

"Why not? I mean, if it were yellow, you'd want to be here more, right?"

Val set her coffee carefully on the table. "Okay, that's it. We need to talk, young lady."

"About what?"

"Whatever it is that's going on in your head. You cannot plot and scheme to get your father and me together." Never mind that she'd done her own share of plotting. It had all been to no avail.

"Why not?" Annie asked, sounding far more curious than daunted.

"Because that's not the way human emotions work. Grown-ups either care about each other or they don't. You can't make things happen just because you'd like them to.'' Val could have attested to that firsthand.

"But Daddy really likes you. I know he does. And you like him. So why can't it work out? Why should we all be miserable, when it would be so easy to be happy?''

Val had wondered the same thing herself until she'd heard Slade proposing marriage solely for the sake of his daughter. They had made love for most of the night. She had experienced a level of passion she had never even known existed. She had honestly thought Slade had, too. Then she'd discovered that she had only convinced him that they'd be compatible enough if he were to marry her for Annie's sake. It was a wonder she hadn't plunged a knife into his heart on the spot.

"It just can't work out," she told Annie very firmly, because it was what she'd finally forced herself to accept. She couldn't spend her whole life with a man who was so insensitive that he didn't even see how deeply he'd insulted her.

"Well, I don't buy it," Annie said stubbornly.

"You don't have to," Val told her. "All that matters is that it's what your father and I both believe."

"Then you're both dumb," Annie proclaimed. She flounced out of her chair and ran to her room.

That was the last Val saw of her until lunchtime. She fixed tuna salad sandwiches, put them on the table and then went to call Annie. She got no response.

Val's stomach knotted. Surely Annie hadn't crawled out a window and run away. She knocked and called out again, then opened the door. Annie was curled up in bed, her back to the door.

Val crossed the room and gazed down at her. She was sound asleep, but her cheeks were still damp with tears.

"Oh, baby," Val whispered and sank onto the edge of the bed. She touched a hand to Annie's cheek.

"Go away," Annie muttered, still half-asleep.

"Lunch is ready."

"I'm not hungry."

"Tuna salad sandwiches and chips," Val said, trying to tempt her. "And I baked cookies. Your favorites." Slade's, too, though she'd sworn as she emptied the bag of chocolate chips into the dough that she was fixing them only for Annie's sake.

"I don't care."

Val bit back a sigh. "Look, sweetie, I know you're unhappy that things aren't going the way you'd hoped, but sometimes we all have disappointments in life."

"Is that all it is to you?" Annie demanded, suddenly quivering with outrage. "A disappointment? Like not getting ice cream for dessert or something? It's my life! I don't have anybody who loves me, not really. Daddy tolerates me because he has to. Grandma and Grandpa dumped me. I thought you were my friend, but you don't care."

"I do care," Val insisted.

"Like I believe that."

"Believe it or not, it's true. Otherwise why do you think I'd be here today?"

"Because Daddy asked you to. He probably paid you."

"Your father is not paying me," she assured the child. "And we both know I'm not very happy with him at the moment, so obviously I'm not doing it for him. So why am I here?"

Annie studied her face. "Because of me," she whispered hesitantly.

"Because of you," Val agreed. "You're a wonderful girl, Annie. You're bright and funny and unpredictable. If I had a little girl, I'd want her to be exactly like you."

"Really?" she asked, hope shining in her eyes.

"Absolutely."

Annie seemed to consider her response for several minutes before her expression brightened. "Okay, then, here's what we do."

Something in her voice alerted Val that she'd blundered in some way she had yet to understand. "Do?" she repeated cautiously.

"Yes," Annie said very firmly. "So you can adopt me and I can be your little girl for real."

Chapter Eleven

For days after Annie's calm declaration that she wanted Val to adopt her, Val couldn't shake the storm of emotions that roared through her. At the time, she'd tried to explain very carefully to Annie why that was impossible, but the conversation continued to nag at her.

Annie had been so serious, so terribly vulnerable. And a part of Val had wanted to say yes. She couldn't deny it. She had come to love Annie already as if she were her own. She blamed Slade's stubborn streak for making that impossible. If only he could have told her he loved her when he'd asked her to marry him, if only it hadn't sounded more like he was striking a bargain than proposing marriage, maybe she would have said yes. Then Annie truly would have been her little girl and Slade would have been her husband. Instead, none of them had what they wanted or needed.

"What do I do?" she asked Laurie. "Do I tell Slade? I mean, this is way beyond her saying she wants to run away from home. She's actually picked out the home she wants to run to."

Laurie regarded her knowingly. "You're flattered, aren't you?"

"Don't be ridiculous."

"You are. A part of you is glad that Annie chose you over Slade. You see it as proof that he's a terrible parent and that you'd be a better one."

"It's not a competition, dammit!"

"No," Laurie agreed mildly. "It's not. Or at least it shouldn't be. You and Slade both want the same thing here. You both want Annie to feel loved and secure."

"That's certainly what I want," Val said. "That's why I've stepped in—to fill in the gaps in her life."

"Oh, really?" Laurie said. "I thought that was more about using Annie to get Slade's attention."

Val stared at her friend. "That's a rotten thing to say."

"Is it?"

Instead of snapping back an answer, Val considered the accusation. "Okay," she admitted reluctantly, "at the beginning, I suppose there might have been some truth to that, but no more. I care about Annie."

"Good. Now we're getting somewhere. And the truth is that Slade's been using you, because he's at a loss about how to handle his daughter. Correct?"

"Yes," Val said, not liking the picture that was emerging of two selfish adults with a ten-year-old caught in the middle.

"Don't look so glum. It's not all bad," Laurie said. "Annie is getting the attention she needs and you and Slade care more about each other than either of you wants to admit."

"Oh, I'll admit it," Val said. "He just doesn't want to hear it." He just wanted a practical marriage of convenience with no messy emotions involved.

"Then back off," Laurie suggested. "Give him time to miss you."

"I thought that was what I was doing," Val said. "Then he came over here and begged me to stay with Annie."

"Obviously this arrangement is way too convenient for him and it's sending very mixed messages to Annie," Laurie said, her expression thoughtful. "I think maybe I was wrong when I said you shouldn't go back to Nashville for a while. I think maybe it's a good idea, after all."

A gut-sick feeling washed over Val. "You're sending me away?"

"Don't look so put out. It was your idea, remember? And it's not Siberia."

"But why now? You just finished telling me a few days ago that you couldn't spare me."

"I was wrong," Laurie said succinctly. "Besides, I think both you and Slade need to remember who you are. You're a career woman, Val. You're the best personal assistant I've ever run across. I know a dozen people who'd snap you up in a heartbeat if I ever let you get away. The last few weeks haven't been typical at all. You've had time on your hands to cater to Slade's every whim and to Annie's." She nodded decisively. "Yes, I think it's for the best. I'm putting you back to work."

Val opened her mouth to argue, then realized that Laurie was probably right. She needed to gain some perspective on everything that had gone on the past few weeks. She'd settled into some sort of fake domesticity, complete with a ready-made family. She needed to weigh that against the life she'd had before Laurie had married Harlan Patrick and they'd started spending most of their time at White Pines.

Could she really juggle both a family and a career and be fair to both? She'd always assumed she could. She'd been instrumental in making Laurie see that she could have it all. Val didn't want to accept it, but maybe the reality was that she would have to choose.

"I'll call the airlines and make the arrangements," she told Laurie. "Then I'll check in with Nick so he can list everything that needs doing to finalize the recording sessions."

"You can take that mountain of fan mail back to Nashville with you, too," Laurie said. "Have the staff there get busy answering it. You've got more important things to do."

More important than being used by a man to play surrogate mother to his lonely little girl, Val told herself firmly. But when the time came to get on the plane, she wasn't nearly as certain that she believed that. Annie had stolen her heart. As for Slade, she was very much afraid that he had captured her soul.

＊　＊　＊

When Annie discovered that Val had gone to Nashville, she was inconsolable. Slade found her huddled in the rocker on the front porch sobbing her eyes out. He guessed she'd already heard the disconcerting news that had reached him just an hour or so earlier. In case he was wrong, he approached the subject cautiously.

"Baby, what's wrong? What happened?" he asked, hunkering down in front of her.

"It's Val," she whispered, sniffing loudly. "I did something wrong and now she's gone away and left me."

Slade had heard all about Val's abrupt departure from Harlan Patrick. His boss seemed to take great pleasure in breaking the news that she'd gone off to Nashville. Nowhere in that discussion had Annie's name come up. Neither had Slade's. In fact, it sounded as if she'd left without giving a thought to either of them.

"Honey, she had work to do. You know she helps Laurie. Sometimes that means she has to go away. It wasn't about you."

"Yes, it was. It's because of what I said."

Slade regarded her with puzzlement. "What did you say that could possibly make Val leave?"

"I told her I wanted her to adopt me," she mumbled, so low he could barely hear the words.

Even so, once they sank in, Slade felt as if the wind had been knocked out of him. He pulled the other rocker close and sat down so he and Annie would be at eye level.

"Tell me exactly what happened."

"I told you. It happened when I was grounded. I said I wanted her to be my mom. She'd said she really liked me, so I figured she'd go for it."

Slade had been through a similar misjudgment all too recently. Apparently neither he nor Annie was good at gauging Val's likely reactions. "Where did I fit into this?" he asked, fearing he knew that answer, too.

Annie gazed down at the floor. "You didn't." Her chin jutted up. "You were mad at me, anyway. I figured you wouldn't care."

"Well, I do," he said forcefully. He reached over and tucked a finger under her chin, forcing her to meet his gaze. "You're my little girl, okay? I know I'm not the best dad in the whole world. I know I've made a lot of mistakes since your mom went away. But I love you, Annie. I wouldn't let you go for anything. I certainly wouldn't let somebody else adopt you and take you away from me, not even Val."

"But she'd be such a great mom," Annie said plaintively.

"I know, baby. I think so, too. But right now it's just you and me. We're stuck with each other. Think we can make it work?" He realized as soon as the words were out just how fearful he was that she'd say no.

"I suppose," she said finally, the lackluster response accompanied by a heavy sigh of resignation.

"How about going into town for ice cream to celebrate?"

"What do we have to celebrate?"

"The fact that we're starting over, that we're a family, just you and me."

Her expression brightened ever so slightly. "Don't you have work to do?"

"It can wait," he said, standing up. "This is more important."

As if she sensed that she had the upper hand for now, she regarded him slyly. "Hot fudge?"

"If that's what you want."

She stood on tiptoe and wrapped her arms around his waist. "I love you, Daddy. I never really wanted to leave you."

"I know, baby. I love you, too." He resolved then and there to make sure she always knew that, no matter what it cost him in time or effort or words. No child of his was ever again going to feel so neglected that she'd rather be adopted than stay with him.

In town, they went straight to Dolan's, where Sharon Lynn greeted them with a look of astonishment. "Playing hooky, Slade?"

He grinned. "Yep, it's a special occasion. I'm out with my best girl."

He knew that for once he'd said the right thing, because Annie's eyes sparkled.

"Well, if it's a celebration, that must call for hot fudge sundaes. Am I right?"

"You bet," Annie said, scrambling onto a stool at the counter.

"You, too, Slade?"

"Why not?"

"So, I hear Val's gone off to Nashville to work on the last-minute details of Laurie's next album. How's my little brother taking the idea of letting his wife go back to Tennessee for recording sessions and then on the road?''

''Haven't heard a complaint out of him,'' Slade said honestly. ''I think your little brother has made his own plans for this tour.''

''Such as?''

''You'll have to ask him,'' he said, not sure if Harlan Patrick had told the whole family the news about Laurie's pregnancy and his intentions to spend the last part of her tour on the road with her.

Sharon Lynn regarded him slyly. ''And how are you doing without Val around?''

''We miss her,'' Annie said. ''Real bad. Don't we, Daddy?''

''I know you do,'' he agreed, and let it go at that. Sharon Lynn's expression suggested she knew perfectly well that he missed Val, too.

''Where's Ashley?'' Annie demanded. ''I thought she usually came to the store with you.''

''She's in the back room taking her nap.'' She glanced up at the clock. ''She'll probably be awake any minute, if you want to check on her.''

''Great,'' Annie said, sliding off her stool. ''Ashley's the best, Daddy. She's real smart. It's almost like having a little sister. Do you think maybe one day—''

''If you're going to check on her, go,'' he said gruffly, cutting her off. He did not want to get into a discussion of babies with Annie, not with a very interested Sharon Lynn listening in. Whatever he said would be all over White Pines by nightfall. Val would hear it right after that.

Sharon Lynn regarded him with sympathy. "Getting a lot of pressure from all sides lately, aren't you?"

"You can say that again." The irony was it was Val they ought to be bugging, not him. He'd asked her to marry him, after all, though he doubted she'd mentioned that to a soul. Everyone clearly thought he was the holdout.

"I'm an Adams, so I can say this—we're a family of meddlers. Don't let us push you into something."

"Not likely," he said curtly.

She laughed. "You say that like you think you'll see the clever wiles and sneaky meddling coming, but, believe me, you won't. Grandpa, particularly, can score a direct hit before you even realize he's in the game."

"I've noticed that," he said. "I'm not worried."

"You're made of tougher stuff, right?" she asked with amusement.

Slade scowled. "Yes."

She patted his hand. "That's what you think."

She slid his sundae in front of him, then went to check on Annie and her own little girl.

Slade took a bite of the ice cream and thick fudge sauce, then sighed and pushed it aside. The only thing sweet he really wanted right now was one of Val's kisses. The best sundae in the world couldn't hold a candle to that. How he was going to convince her of that, though, was beyond him.

A few days after the debacle with the paint and the adoption scheme, when Annie asked Slade if she could help him, he was more open to the idea. Not that he could imagine her being of much assistance, but at least he'd know firsthand what she was up to. He also knew she was feeling very much at loose ends since Val had left town.

"I'm getting ready to muck out the stalls," he informed her, figuring that would put her desire to be like him to the ultimate test. "Are you sure you want to help?"

To his astonishment, her eyes brightened. "You'll really let me?"

He hesitated, then shrugged. "Sure. Why not?" He gave her terse directions, then stood back and watched as she threw herself into the task with energetic enthusiasm. She was a constant source of amazement to him.

"Hey, Dad," she called after she had thoroughly cleaned two stalls and left them spotless.

"What?"

"Do you suppose you could teach me to ride sometime?" she asked hesitantly. The wary expression in her eyes suggested she was prepared to be rebuffed, and the tilt of her chin hinted that she wouldn't take it lightly.

He considered the out-of-the-blue request and wondered what had brought it on. "You were never interested in riding before," he noted.

She stood in front of him, her expression serious. "But you love it, don't you? I mean, even after the accident and all, you still love the horses. You didn't, like, go off and become a mechanic like Grandpa or something.''

Slade cringed at the very idea of an indoor job. His father might think engines were every bit as fascinating as an animal, but he didn't. ''No way.''

''Well, then, I figure, if you like horses so much, I should, too. It's gotta be in my genes, right?''

Slade considered Val's assessment weeks ago that his daughter was interested in tools because he was. Then he thought back to the saddle he'd seen Annie admiring and wondered if that was part of the same phenomenon. Was Annie reaching out to him in the only ways she knew how? Was she struggling to fit into his life by doing the things he did, so they could share in the enjoyment? And if that was it, wasn't it way past time he met her halfway?

''Put down that rake and come with me,'' he said.

Her eyes widened. ''Why?''

He grinned. ''Because you're about to have your first riding lesson, young lady.''

''On Black Knight?'' she asked hopefully. ''He's so awesome.''

''Nope. I think he's a little too feisty for you. We'll start with Aunt Sadie.''

''But she's old,'' Annie protested, obviously disappointed.

''She's gentle,'' Slade corrected. ''That's what matters. She won't dump you in the dust the first time you get on.''

Annie actually looked as if she wouldn't mind being bounced from the saddle if it meant getting to ride a more challenging horse than the old mare, but

Slade remained firm. He brought Aunt Sadie out of her stall and showed Annie how to saddle her and put on her bridle.

When the horse was ready, Annie led her out of the barn and into the corral.

"I'll give you a boost up," Slade said, linking his hands for Annie to step into. She mounted the horse as smoothly as if she'd done it many times. "Are you sure you've never been on a horse before?"

"Never," she said. "But I used to climb onto the fence rail at Grandma's and pretend it was a horse. I got pretty good at getting on."

Amused, Slade nodded. "You're good, all right. Now let's see how you are at riding the real thing."

He took the lead and moved around the corral in a slow circle. "How does it feel?"

"Boring," Annie said. "I want to ride fast."

"First things first." He handed her the reins. "Let's see you get her to start and stop."

Aunt Sadie had a very docile nature, so there was almost nothing Annie could have done to get her riled up enough to throw off her rider. But somewhere in the back of the old mare's mind must have lurked a memory of a time when she'd run as fast as the wind. At Annie's urging, she broke into a full gallop before Slade realized what was going on.

As the horse tore past him, he shouted at Annie, "Pull on the reins, sweetie! Get her to stop."

Either Annie didn't hear him or chose to ignore the command—more likely the latter. Her face was split with a grin as she sailed past for the second time.

"Annie Sutton, you're going to spend a month in

your room if you don't ride that horse over here and get off of it right now,'' he yelled.

He wasn't sure when he finally realized that something was wrong. Maybe it was when Aunt Sadie broke toward the open gate at the back of the corral. Maybe it was when he caught Annie's smile fading and panic settling onto her face.

''Daddy!'' she squealed. ''I can't make her stop.''

Slade broke into a run, but with his bum leg he was no match for the horse, who'd sensed a kindred spirit and was intent on showing Annie what she was made of.

''Whoa!'' Annie shouted to no avail. ''Daddy! Help!''

''Pull slowly on the reins,'' Slade advised, trying to remain calm.

Annie did as he said, but she was so panicked that she was digging her heels into the horse's sides at the same time, sending Aunt Sadie a mixed message. The horse made her own decision about which message to listen to.

When she reached the gate, Aunt Sadie bolted through and took off for open pastures, Annie clinging to her back. Her sobs carried on the breeze, filling Slade with a terrible sense of helplessness and dread.

Harlan Patrick heard the commotion and came running. He took in the situation at a glance, grabbed Black Knight's mane and threw himself onto the horse bareback. Slade realized that's what he should have done, but everything had unfolded so quickly he hadn't had time to think. He cursed the injuries that made his reflexes too slow to have done what Harlan Patrick was able to do without thought.

He watched the huge black stallion eat up the ground between him and Aunt Sadie. When he was close enough, Harlan Patrick grabbed the reins of the runaway horse and slowed her down. The instant Aunt Sadie halted, he reached over and gathered Annie into his arms and brought her back.

"Thank you," Slade said, taking Annie from him. Still sobbing, she clung to Slade's neck and wrapped her legs around his waist.

"I'll see to the horses," Harlan Patrick said. "She'll be fine, Slade. It happens to every kid at some point. Don't beat yourself up."

"She could have been killed," Slade said grimly.

"But she wasn't. That's what matters. She's fine. The horses are fine. No harm done."

Except to Slade's pride. He felt like he'd failed his daughter one more time. Her first ride, which should have been a wonderful memory, would probably haunt her now.

He realized then that Annie had grown silent. He turned his head and met her gaze.

"I'm sorry, Daddy."

"It wasn't your fault."

"It must have been. You said she was gentle. I must have done something wrong."

"No, baby. Sometimes horses just get an idea into their heads. That's why you have to take it easy and learn how to control them. Next time will be better."

Eyes shimmering with tears suddenly filled with hope. "You'll let me ride again?"

Much as he wanted to deny her the chance and keep her from risk, he nodded. "If you want to."

"Oh, yes," she breathed, her face lit with excitement. "Up until I couldn't get her to stop, it was awesome."

Slade shook his head. "I guess you were right about those genes of mine being part of your makeup. I never took a spill so bad that I didn't want to get right back on and try it again."

"See, Daddy? We *are* alike."

As humbled as he was by how obviously thrilled Annie was by the comparison, Slade couldn't honestly say if he thought the assessment was good or bad.

Chapter Twelve

Back in Nashville Val worked from dawn to way past dusk, driven by a need to fill every hour with so much work that there wouldn't be a single second when her thoughts could stray to an impossible cowboy and his tomboy daughter. The tactic worked reasonably effectively, though Nick had taken to steering clear of her because she snapped his head off at the slightest provocation.

"If you're so damn miserable, go back to Texas," Laurie's agent told her at one point. "I don't know what it is about the men down there, but neither you nor Laurie seem to have a lick of common sense when they're involved."

"There's work to be done here," she'd retorted, ignoring his analysis of the potent impact of Texas males. "Laurie thought it would be best if I helped you out for a while and that's exactly what I'm doing."

"Fine," he'd said, relenting. "Far be it from me to question the wisdom of my biggest star, but if you ask me, we'd all be happier if you'd just give in and work things out with the cowboy. She certainly was."

"Nobody asked you."

Nick had shrugged, then gone back into his office and slammed the door. Val had no doubt that if it had been up to him, he'd have sent her packing. He'd never been crazy about the influence she had over his superstar. Nor had he liked the fact that she'd helped Laurie keep the secret of her first pregnancy from him. He had told them both in no uncertain terms that if they kept him in the dark on anything that important ever again, he'd cut his professional ties with Laurie. Val's present mood only added to the ongoing friction.

The days passed, filled with brusque encounters with Nick and a million and one details to be handled. Slade never—well, hardly ever—entered her thoughts.

But there was nothing Val could do to prevent Slade from haunting her dreams. She was having an especially sweet one when the ringing of the phone woke her.

"Hey, sleepyhead, I thought you'd be up with the chickens," Laurie said cheerfully.

"You're the one on the farm," Val grumbled, burying her head in the pillow.

"It's a ranch."

"Same difference."

"Not exactly, but we'll let that pass."

"Why are you calling at this hour?" she muttered. "It's still dark out."

"Something's happened," Laurie said, her tone suddenly sobering. "Harlan Patrick and I debated whether to tell you, but I thought you'd want to know. And since I was up anyway, I figured I'd try to catch you at home."

Heart pounding, Val sat upright at once. "Is it Slade?" she asked, instantly alert. "Has he been hurt?"

"No, though I find it interesting that you're so worried about a man you'd vowed to put out of your mind."

"If it's not Slade, then it has to be Annie," Val said, ignoring the taunt. "What's happened, Laurie? Spit it out. She hasn't run away again, has she?"

"Okay, yes, it's Annie. And, no, she hasn't run away. She is not hurt, either, but she had a few terrifying moments." She went on to describe the riding lesson that had gone awry. "I'm not sure which one of them was more shaken, Annie or Slade. He's absolutely beside himself that it was Harlan Patrick who thought to jump on Black Knight and go after her. Harlan Patrick's worried about him. He told me Slade feels like he failed her again."

"That's ridiculous."

"Well, of course it is, but you know Slade. All that macho pride has kicked in."

"I'm coming back," Val said, making up her mind

at once. "I'll check the flights the second we hang up and let you know when I'll be there."

"I think a phone call would do the trick," Laurie suggested dryly. "It would mean a lot to Annie to know that you're concerned about her."

"No," Val said firmly, thinking as much of father as daughter. A call wouldn't settle anything with Slade. "A call's not good enough. I need to be there. Those two will probably retreat into silence again unless somebody's there to keep them talking."

"They were talking just fine last time I saw them. They had their heads together planning Annie's next riding lesson. Slade relented and said she could try again, even though he's obviously not happy about it."

"It might not last," Val said, though her position was clearly weakened by Laurie's reassurance.

"In other words, your mind is made up and you don't want me bothering you with facts," Laurie said, chuckling. "You've only been gone a few days. You weren't, by any chance, just waiting for an excuse to come back?"

Maybe she had been, Val admitted to herself, though not to Laurie. Work wasn't nearly as fulfilling as it had once been. And Nashville hadn't felt nearly as much like home as she'd expected when she'd returned. Apparently, for better or for worse, she truly had left her heart in Texas.

"You're not still beating yourself up over Annie's accident, are you?" Harlan Patrick asked when Slade wandered into the barn at midmorning.

Slade hadn't especially wanted to be reminded of the accident or his own guilt-ridden reaction to it. "Nope."

"Because it wasn't your fault." Harlan Patrick went on as if Slade hadn't spoken.

"I know," Slade conceded. "Could have happened to anybody, anytime."

"Exactly," his boss said, as enthusiastically as if Slade had grasped a very tricky concept.

"Did you want something?" Slade asked, hoping to get him to move on.

"Not really," Harlan Patrick said. He turned to leave, then paused. "By the way, did I happen to mention that Val is coming back today? She should be here anytime now."

Slade came very close to gouging a huge chunk of skin out of his hand, when the pick he was using to clean Black Knight's shoes slipped. "Is that so?" he responded, as if the news were of no consequence. After she'd left, he'd half wondered if she would ever set foot in Texas again. He'd had the uncomfortable feeling that he'd driven her away.

"Thought you'd want to know." Harlan Patrick waited expectantly.

"And now I do," Slade said tersely.

Harlan Patrick chuckled. "You are so pitiful. You know you want to ask why she's coming back so fast."

Because he did, Slade continued to pretend indifference. "Do I?"

"It's because of Annie," Harlan Patrick supplied.

Slade's gaze shot up. "Annie didn't go calling her, did she?"

"Nope, you can thank my wife for the phone call. She reported all the details about Annie's accident, including the fact that your daughter is just fine. Val decided she needed to see for herself."

Slade wasn't sure why that aggravated him, but it did. It was more proof that Val cared as deeply as a mother would about his little girl. Yet she refused to make the role official. That meant her rejection of his proposal had everything to do with him.

But, dammit, if he didn't measure up, why hadn't she just said so? Why had she slept with him in the first place? It seemed to him the woman didn't know her own mind. He could have worked up a pretty good head of steam on the subject, but the lady in question came wandering into the barn just then. His pulse started pounding as if he'd been wrestling a bull for an hour.

"Speak of the devil," Harlan Patrick said, sweeping Val off her feet and planting a kiss on her forehead. "Welcome home. We sure did miss you around here, didn't we, Slade?"

Slade grunted a noncommittal response that had Harlan Patrick grinning.

"Guess I'll go on up to the house and check on my wife, unless you two need me to stick around for some reason." He regarded first Val and then Slade expectantly. "No? I didn't think so. See you two. Play nice."

After he'd gone, Slade muttered, "He is a very annoying man."

"I think he's wonderful," Val said.

"Something else we can fight about, I suppose."

Val sighed. "I didn't come back to fight with you. How's Annie?"

"Annie is just fine. I'm surprised you're not up at my place checking her for bumps and bruises."

She grinned. "I would have been, but she wasn't around." Her expression sobered. "How are you? You must have been terrified when the horse took off."

"I've had better moments," Slade agreed. He sat back on his haunches and surveyed her as intently as if he hadn't seen her in months, rather than days. "I see you're back in your fancy shoes again. Must be the big-city influence. You never did seem real comfortable as a ranch girl."

"Are you deliberately trying to bait me?" she asked, sounding more curious than angry.

"Why would I do that?"

"I have to wonder the same thing. You didn't, by any chance, miss me?"

"Not me. Too much work to do."

"I missed you," she said softly, her voice filled with what might have been regret.

Slade fixed her with a steady gaze. "Is that so? You don't seem especially happy about it."

"Why would I be? We're on different wavelengths, that's plain enough. You seem intent on keeping us that way."

His gaze shot up at the unreasonable accusation. "Not me. I wanted to marry you, remember?"

"Oh, yeah, I remember. That proposal was one of

the more memorable moments of my life,'' she said with unmistakable sarcasm. She headed for the door. ''I'd better go.''

Slade stood up and took a step toward her. ''Val?''

She hesitated.

''Don't go.''

She slowly turned back. ''Why?''

''Because I did miss you,'' he confessed, unable to hide the bemusement he felt. It was ridiculous to miss a woman he considered to be little more than a thorn in his side. ''And if I wouldn't get a slap for it, I might show you just how much.''

She seemed to be weighing that, but as his breath lodged in his throat, she took a step toward him, then halted. ''Meet me halfway,'' she taunted.

Slade stepped closer and took her shoulders in his hands. She was so fragile he feared she'd break, but he knew deep down that she was tougher than he was by a long shot. Gazing into her eyes, he felt his senses spinning out of control. Desire slammed through him, unbidden. Mostly unwanted.

Still, he couldn't keep himself from lowering his head until his mouth found hers. Fire exploded through him at the first touch. To his amazement, she was trembling in his arms, and when he looked, there was a suspicious sheen to her eyes.

''You aren't about to cry, are you?'' he asked worriedly.

She blinked rapidly. Her chin jutted up. ''Why would I cry over a silly kiss?''

''That's what I'd like to know.'' He dismissed the

fact that she'd just referred to the kiss as silly. Otherwise, he might have been insulted.

"I'm not shedding any tears over you, Slade Sutton," she said with a touch of defiance. "So you can keep that ego of yours in check."

This time when she whirled around to leave, Slade didn't try to stop her. He just stood back and enjoyed the view of her sashaying along on those ridiculously high heels. He'd been telling himself for days now that he didn't give a damn that she'd gone. Now he was forced to admit that he was very glad that she was back. For the last half hour or so, he'd finally felt whole again.

Blasted man, Val thought to herself as she wandered off in search of Annie, after stopping long enough to change back into boots and jeans. Telling her she belonged in the city, that she didn't fit in on a ranch. Well, he could just go to blazes. She had as much right to be here as he did. She had a job here, just like he did. She had friends. She could even learn about cows, if she was of a mind to.

"Val, you're back!"

Annie came racing toward her and all but threw herself into Val's arms. Val stumbled back at the impact, but she couldn't stop the grin that spread across her face at the exuberant welcome. At least one member of the Sutton family knew her own heart and wasn't afraid to let her emotions show.

"Hold still and let me get a good look at you," Val instructed.

"I almost got thrown from a horse," Annie said proudly. "Did you hear?"

"I heard."

"Harlan Patrick saved me."

"I heard that, too."

"Daddy looked like he was going to faint. He was real scared."

"I'm sure he was."

"You know what, though?"

"What?"

"He said it was okay for me to ride again. He's going to give me another lesson this afternoon. Want to watch?" she demanded excitedly. "I'm going to star in a rodeo just like Daddy one day."

Val winced. She doubted Slade was privy to that particular bit of career planning on his daughter's part. "Have you mentioned that to your father yet?"

"Not exactly. I figured I'd better get really good before I tell him. Otherwise, he'll just say no."

"A few weeks ago you wanted to be an Olympic diver. What happened to that?"

"I'm still diving," Annie said, clearly perplexed. "Why can't I do both?"

Val laughed. "I suppose you can, if that's what you want. Of course, you've only been on a horse once. What makes you think you'll really like being in the rodeo?"

"Because Daddy did," she said simply.

"You know, kiddo, you don't have to do everything your dad did."

"But I want to," Annie protested.

"Because you really enjoy it, or because you think it will make him love you more?"

She could see from the look on Annie's face that she hadn't expected anyone else to understand her motivations. Maybe she hadn't even recognized them herself until Val put it into words.

"I want him to see that I'm really like him, not like my mom," Annie said.

"The point is to be Annie," Val said. "That's what he'll love you for. Not for trying to be someone else."

Annie didn't seem convinced by the logic. "Will you come watch me ride or not?"

"I'll come," Val said. That way there'd be two people standing by the corral railing with their hearts in their throats. "What time?"

"Not till five, 'cause Daddy has to finish work first." She bounced up and down excitedly. "That means there's time for us to go into town and have pizza, if you want to. Zack and Josh could meet us, maybe."

"Why not?" Val agreed. "Check with your father first."

Annie ran off, then came back waving money. "He said okay, but he's paying."

Since he wasn't there to argue with, Val nodded. "Let's go, then. Where are Zack and Josh?"

"At the vet clinic with Dani. She's paying them to help out."

"Then we'll go by there."

"Or I could call them on your cell phone," Annie suggested. "I've never used one before."

Val grinned at her enthusiasm. "It's in my purse."

Annie dragged out the phone, followed Val's instructions, then beamed when the call went through. "Hey, Zack, guess what? I'm on Val's cell phone and we're in the car."

Val couldn't hear the boy's response, but assumed from Annie's expression that he was duly impressed. Wouldn't it be wonderful if life could always be so uncomplicated? she thought to herself, listening to one side of the conversation. Instead, grown-ups carried all sorts of baggage that interfered with taking pleasure in the simple things.

Take Slade, for instance. He would never in a million years admit that being dumped by his ex-wife had scarred him so deeply he was afraid to love again, but that was exactly what was going on. If asked, he'd probably just say Suzanne had been a jerk and that their split had been for the best. Val thought she knew better. He'd really loved her. Otherwise her leaving wouldn't have bothered him half as much as it clearly did after all this time. It wouldn't have left him incapable of admitting how he felt about another woman. The idea that he had been capable of loving so deeply once gave her hope for their own future.

"Hey, Val," Annie said, poking her sharply in the ribs.

"What?" she murmured.

"You just drove past the clinic."

Dragging her attention back to the present, Val realized she'd driven halfway through Los Piños without even noticing. Thinking about Slade had a way of distracting her. She glanced in the rearview mirror and saw the twins standing on the sidewalk in front of the clinic, looking baffled over being passed by.

"Sorry," she murmured, going around the next block and heading back.

"You were thinking about Daddy, weren't you?" Annie inquired, her expression smug.

"What makes you think that?"

"Because you looked all dreamy one minute and mad the next."

Out of the mouths of babes, Val thought wryly. The child had nailed it. That was exactly the way Slade made her feel.

"You know what I think?" Annie asked.

Val was afraid to ask. "What?" she inquired cautiously.

"Since you said you wouldn't adopt me, I think that you and Daddy should get married. Then you could be my mom. It would be great," Annie enthused, obviously sold on the idea. "We get along great and you almost never yell at me. You said you'd like to have a little girl just like me, so why not me, right?"

What was it with the Suttons? Val thought. They both seemed to think marriage was about instant motherhood. Fortunately, she was in front of the clinic and Josh and Zack were scrambling into the back seat.

"We'll discuss it another time," she told Annie firmly.

"But you do think it's a good idea, don't you?" the girl persisted.

"Another time," she repeated.

"What arc you talking about?" Zack demanded, his freckled face alight with curiosity.

"And how come you drove right past us before?" Josh asked.

"She was distracted," Annie confided. "She was thinking about Daddy."

Heat flooded Val's face. If she didn't change the subject and fast, this story was going to spread through the Adams clan with the speed and intensity of a wildfire.

"What do you guys want on your pizza?" she asked, figuring that most little boys would rather discuss food than mushy stuff any day. She hadn't counted on the Adams penchant for matchmaking. Obviously it took hold at a very early age and even influenced those connected to the family only by marriage.

"You're in love with Slade?" Josh asked.

"Uh-huh," Annie answered for her.

"Wow, that's neat," Zack said. "You'd be, like, Annie's mom then, huh?"

"Okay, enough," Val said, pulling into a parking space in front of the Italian restaurant. "This is not open for discussion." She scowled first at Annie, then at both boys. "Are we clear?"

Zack looked knowingly at Josh. "She's got it bad, all right. Remember when Dad used that exact same voice to tell us to keep our noses out of his relationship with Dani?"

"That's right," Josh said. "He was always telling us to mind our own business. It was a good thing we didn't, though. Otherwise, they might never had gotten married.'' He looked at Annie. ''Sometimes grown-ups are real slow about stuff like this. You gotta give 'em a push.''

Val moaned. ''There will be no pushing, no meddling, no discussion,'' she said flatly. ''Otherwise, there will be no pizza.''

That finally shut them up. But she could tell from the grins they exchanged that as far as they were concerned, the matter was far from ended.

Chapter Thirteen

Val the cowgirl was back with a vengeance. Slade watched her heading toward the corral with a sinking sensation in the pit of his stomach. Her snug jeans gave him almost as many ideas as those heels she'd abandoned in favor of more practical boots. Still feminine to the core, though, she'd knotted her Western-style shirt at the waist. He knew from past observation that if she lifted her arms just a little, the hem of that shirt would glide up and expose a tantalizing few inches of silky skin. His body tightened just anticipating it.

"What bee have you got in your bonnet?" he asked when she neared.

"We have to talk," she declared, in the kind of no-nonsense tone that always had the contradictory effect of making him think of everything except the business that was clearly on her mind.

"About?"

"Annie."

Val began striding up and down in front of him at a dizzying pace. Slade reached out and snagged her arm in an attempt to get her attention.

"Whoa now! Why is it that when I want to talk about what's best for Annie, you act like I'm insulting you? Now you can't wait to bring up the subject."

Val frowned. "There's a problem. Do you want to hear about it or not?" She took up pacing again.

"Experience tells me I'd be better off not knowing, but go ahead."

She paused briefly and declared, "Annie's decided she wants me for a mother."

"No news there," he said. "She wanted you to adopt her not so long ago."

"Are you going to listen or not?"

He held up his hands in a gesture of surrender. "Okay. I'll be quiet as a mouse. Just be sure to cue me when it's my turn. Otherwise I might miss it."

She frowned at his attempt at humor. "Very funny. Now here's what we're up against. She has gotten Josh and Zack on her side. I wouldn't be one bit surprised if they weren't up at the main house plotting with Harlan."

That was actually the best news Slade had had in weeks, but he could see that Val wasn't overjoyed about it. She'd gone back to her agitated pacing.

"And the problem is?" he inquired, just to rile her. He knew perfectly well what the problem was. She was tempted and she really hated it that she was. She'd vowed to resist him till doomsday and she was scared spitless that she was going to cave in long before that.

"She's going to be disappointed," she declared, chin jutted up.

"Is she?"

"You know she is," Val said, scowling at him. "We've already decided it won't work between us. You need to stop her before she has her hopes dashed."

Slade gave her a pitying look. "You know, for a woman who claims to know my daughter better than I do, you really don't have a clue what she's like, do you? She's not going to be put off by anything I say." He paused thoughtfully, then gave Val a pointed look. "She's a lot like you in that respect. She'll pester us both until she gets her way. I say we give in and save ourselves the trouble."

"She is not going to get her way," Val said grimly. "We decided—"

Slade cut her off. "You decided."

"Same difference."

"No, sweetheart, it is not the same difference. You have your agenda. I have mine. Much as I hate to disappoint you, I'm on Annie's side on this one."

She stopped her pacing and stared at him. "You are?"

"Oh, yes."

"But why? We agreed—"

"No," he corrected again. "You refused my proposal. *We* didn't agree about anything. Of course, there's no news there, either. We haven't agreed about much since the day we met. Keeps things interesting.''

''Oh, for heaven's sakes, we're playing word games,'' she snapped irritably. ''The point is we're not getting married. Annie shouldn't get her hopes up.''

Slade shrugged. ''Why not? I have.''

Her gaze narrowed. ''You have?''

''Sure. In fact, I've found the past few minutes very encouraging.''

She regarded him with a baffled expression. ''You have? Why?''

''You're fighting me too hard on this. You came running back from Nashville the minute you heard Annie had a little scare. You might as well stop denying it. You're involved with us, darlin'. That gives me hope.''

''Well, of course I'm involved with you. That's not the point.''

''Then what is?''

The simple question silenced her.

''Well?'' he prodded.

''If you don't get it, then I am not about to explain it to you,'' she said with a huff of indignation. ''But for the record, I will not marry you, Slade. That's final.''

''We'll see,'' he retorted mildly. For the first time in ages, he actually thought he might have a chance with her. He just had to be a little patient. Maybe let Annie work on her.

''You're pitiful, Sutton,'' he said, when Val was

out of earshot. "You're counting on a ten-year-old to do your courting for you."

The sorry truth was, though, that Annie was probably a whole lot more adept at it than he was.

"You know, that gal of yours is smart as a whip," Harlan Adams told Slade when the rancher wandered down to the corral the next morning to watch Black Knight's workout. He'd been stopping by almost daily lately.

"Val?" The name slipped out before Slade could stop it.

The old man chuckled. "I was talking about your daughter, but Val's a bright one, too." He studied Slade intently. "Annie seems to think the two of you would make a good match. How do you feel about that?"

"Truthfully, I've had thoughts along that line myself," Slade surprised himself by admitting. A few months ago he wouldn't have shared personal information with anyone. Now he'd concluded that a little matchmaking expertise from a grand master would be more than welcome.

"Well, what's stopping you, then?" Harlan asked impatiently. "The woman's had eyes for you ever since she set foot on this ranch. Nobody around here's missed that."

Now that he was into the subject, Slade decided to lay all his cards on the table. "To tell you the truth, I made a couple of tactical mistakes. I haven't been able to recover from them yet."

Harlan's eyes took on the excited glint of a man

rising to a challenge. He hoisted himself up onto a railing, clearly settling down to listen. "Tell me," he commanded.

Slade described how he'd reached the conclusion that Val would be the perfect mother for Annie.

"And you told her that?"

"Yes."

"And that's when you asked her to marry you?"

Slade nodded, wincing under the old man's incredulous look.

"Whoo-ee, I'm surprised she left you standing."

"To be honest, so am I. She wasn't happy, that's for sure."

"Well, can you blame her? No woman wants to sign on as mother for a kid without getting a little something for herself in the bargain. If raising a child's all she wants, she could hire on as a housekeeper or open a day-care center, and be done with it. That's not Val's style. Any fool could see that."

"Well, I missed it," Slade said defensively. "At least, until it was too late to take the words back."

Harlan subjected him to a penetrating stare. "Is this still all about Annie?"

"No. The minute Val stormed out, I realized I loved her."

Harlan gave a little nod of satisfaction. "Good. Now we're getting somewhere. Why haven't you just flat out told her?"

"After what's happened, she'd never believe me. She'd figure I was saying all the right words, just to get my way."

The rancher's expression turned thoughtful. "You

could be right about that. Timing's important in a situation like this. So, if words won't do it, you'll have to take action.''

"Such as?''

"Prove to her how much you care. Court her, Son. Flowers, candy, the whole nine yards. I've seen some mighty fine courtships around this ranch in my time. Been party to a few of them. You just have to listen real close and do exactly what I tell you.''

"Won't that seem a little obvious?''

"More than likely, at least at first. You'll have to prove you're in it for the long haul. Never let up. Don't give her a second's peace. Sweet-talk her every chance you get. Worked on Janet and she was a tough one, let me tell you.''

"I'm afraid sweet talk's not in my nature,'' Slade objected.

"You'll learn, Son. When the stakes are high enough, a man can do most anything.''

"What stakes?'' Annie demanded, slipping up behind them, her face alight with curiosity. "Are you gonna play poker? Will you teach me?''

"Poker's a game for grown-ups, young lady,'' Harlan told her. "But when you're old enough, I'll teach you how to play and win. Right now, though, your daddy and I are talking about something else.''

"Val, I'll bet.'' She grinned up at Harlan. "Thanks.''

He reached down and ruffled her hair. "Glad to help out. You here for your riding lesson?''

She nodded. "Want to stay and watch?''

"Afraid not. I've got to get back up to the house

before Janet gets home. I might be able to sneak a cup of real coffee and a couple of Maritza's sugar cookies without getting caught.'' He winked at Slade. ''You remember what I told you and keep me posted on what's happening. Sometimes a plan requires a few adjustments before it starts to work.''

Slade shook his hand. ''Thank you, sir. I won't forget.''

''See that you don't. I haven't had a failure yet. I don't aim to start now.''

After his boss had headed back to the main house, Slade noticed Annie grinning from ear to ear. ''You sent him down here, didn't you?'' he demanded.

''What if I did?'' she asked defiantly. ''Somebody had to do something. If I wait around for you and Val, I'll be too old to even need a mother.''

''Thanks,'' Slade said, clearly catching her by surprise.

Prepared to make her case, she seemed startled by his response. ''You're not mad?''

''No, though as a general rule, we don't go around sharing our private business with outsiders.''

''Grandpa Harlan's not an outsider.''

''He is not your grandfather,'' Slade pointed out.

''But he said I could call him that, so that makes him practically family, right?''

Annie's convoluted logic silenced him.

''Well?'' she prodded.

''Close enough, I guess.'' Slade waved her toward the barn. ''Go on and bring your horse out and saddle her up.''

''By myself?'' she asked, eyes wide.

"You've got to learn sometime."

"Oh, wow," she said, and took off running.

"Slow down," Slade hollered, but he was wasting his breath. Annie never did anything slower than full throttle.

He realized as he waited for her to return that the two of them were actually settling into a workable routine these days. They were communicating, something he hadn't thought possible a few weeks ago. And though she still occasionally mystified him, he found the unexpected twists her mind took to be fascinating, rather than terrifying. He supposed he had Val to thank for that.

"Daddy, is this okay?" she asked tentatively, bringing out the saddled mare. Aunt Sadie stood docilely beside her.

Slade checked the cinch, tightened it ever so slightly, then gave his daughter's shoulder a squeeze. "Good job."

Her eyes lit up. "Really? I did it right?"

"Just about perfect. Now let's see you mount," he said, holding out his hands to give her a boost up.

"Not bad," he said approvingly. "You're getting better every day."

"Pretty soon you can start teaching me stuff you did in the rodeo," she said.

Slade froze. "No," he said curtly. "The rodeo's not for you."

"Why not? You did it."

"And look how I ended up."

"You didn't get hurt in the rodeo," she said, refusing to back down. "You got hurt in the accident."

"Forget it," Slade snapped. "It's no life for a girl."

Tears welled up in Annie's eyes at his sharp tone. He sighed heavily, then muttered, "Sorry, I didn't mean to yell."

"Why did you?"

"Because the rodeo is dangerous," he explained. "I want you to do something different with your life, something safe and sensible."

"And boring," she said derisively.

Slade fought to control his temper. Fighting her on this now would only make her cling to the idea all the tighter. He could see that she wanted to live up to his example, mostly because that was the only one she had. That made it all the more critical to get Val in her life, so she'd realize there were options for women that didn't involve potentially life-threatening confrontations with nasty-tempered broncs or bulls. Though he'd known many brilliantly skilled women on the rodeo circuit, it wasn't what he wanted for his daughter.

"We'll discuss it when you're older," he said finally.

"How old?"

"Ninety-seven," he teased, forcing a grin.

"Oh, Daddy," she said, but she grinned back at him. "I love you."

"I love you, too, angel." Even as the words crossed his lips, he realized it was one of the very few times he'd told her since the first few days of her life, when he'd been overwhelmed with the emotions of being a new father. Maybe if he practiced saying the words to Annie, they'd feel more comfortable when the time came to try them out on Val.

Watching Slade working with Annie, seeing the girl's eyes shining from all the fatherly attention, Val sighed.

"Your job here is done," Laurie observed, joining her on the porch. "You've gotten the two of them together."

"They do seem easier around each other, don't they?"

"They've become a family," Laurie said. "Now, then, what about the two of you? Before you give me some evasive answer, understand that I am not asking about you and Annie, I'm asking about you and Slade."

Val hesitated. "Nothing's changed."

"I don't understand it. The man is obviously crazy about you. Why hasn't he done something about it?"

"Actually, he did ask me to marry him," Val admitted unhappily, finally prepared to spill the whole story. Maybe her friend could explain where it had all gone wrong.

A beaming smile spread across Laurie's face. "That's wonderful." At Val's silence, her expression faltered. "Isn't it? I thought you loved him."

"I do."

Laurie shook her head. "I don't get it."

"He still wants me just for Annie's sake."

"Still?"

"It came up before. I turned him down," she said

succinctly. "I told him his proposal was insulting. I haven't changed my mind."

"Are you sure this is all about Annie? The man doesn't strike me as the type who'd saddle himself with a wife he didn't care about just for the sake of his child. Maybe he just doesn't know how to admit he loves you, especially after fighting you so hard. It's a male pride thing."

Val wanted to believe that Laurie was right, but what if she wasn't? "What am I supposed to do?" she demanded. "Take a risk and marry him and pray that he'll get around to admitting it one of these days? Sorry. I don't live that dangerously."

Laurie looked disappointed in her. "I can't believe it. Is this the same woman who was pushing and prodding me into marrying Harlan Patrick and working out the details of our living arrangements later? I guess it's a whole lot easier to dole out advice than it is to take it."

"That was different," Val insisted, not rising to the bait. "You two were wild about each other. You had been practically forever. The details were just that— details. Love—or the lack of it—is the core issue between Slade and me. He claims he doesn't believe in it. He says we're compatible enough and I'll be good for Annie. That's it."

"Forget what he says," Laurie declared impatiently. "You should know by now that actions speak louder. From where I sit, and believe me, I've been on the sidelines through most of this, I say the man loves you. I've watched him these past few months, Val. He never takes his eyes off of you."

"Probably because he's trying to figure out where I'll pop up next so he can avoid being there," she grumbled. "I don't want to spend a lifetime with a man who's not totally committed from the outset. Things get complicated enough during a marriage even when there is a strong basis of love to start with."

"Val," Laurie chided. "I have never known you to resist a challenge. How can you walk away from one that's this important to your whole future?"

Val didn't have an answer for her.

Laurie regarded her with quiet intensity, then asked, "Or have you decided that Slade Sutton is just not worth it?"

Laurie's words echoed in Val's head for days to come, along with Annie's pleas to stop by for another cooking lesson. In fact, both Annie and Laurie seemed to be scheming to throw Val and Slade together as often as possible. Val was having a hard time avoiding all the traps they laid. Even Harlan Adams seemed to be getting in on the act, which terrified her. She knew precisely how relentless he could be when he'd deemed a match to be suitable.

She stubbornly resisted all their efforts. She didn't want to discuss Slade, didn't want to discuss her own cowardice. In fact, she didn't want to do much of anything except stay in her room and mope. That pretty much kept her out of Slade's path as well, which she was convinced was the only way to make him entirely happy.

She was surprised, therefore, when he turned up at

Harlan Patrick and Laurie's one night wearing a suit and carrying a bouquet of flowers.

"What are you doing here?" she asked suspiciously, as Laurie and her husband hovered in the background, unrepentantly eavesdropping.

"I've come courting." His expression practically dared her to make something of that.

Her pulse leaped despite her very recent determination to put this man entirely out of her life. "Why?"

He grinned at that. "The usual reasons. You know, man meets woman, man's hormones kick in and the next thing he knows he's doing things that are totally out of character, like dressing up on a week night and buying posies." He held them out to her, looking awkward as a schoolboy on a first date.

"I see," she said, reluctantly accepting the bouquet, which was fragrant with roses from Janet's garden. "You must have missed the all-important lesson about calling and asking for a date."

"Nope," he said without the slightest hint of apology. "I deliberately skipped right on over that part. I figured you might turn me down. Annie says the unexpected could work to my advantage."

Val held back a chuckle. "You're taking courting advice from a ten-year-old?"

He ran a finger inside his collar, as if it were suddenly too tight. Patches of red stained his cheeks. "She seems to have a better grasp of this stuff than I do. It's been a long time since I've played the game. Haven't much wanted to until now."

For some reason—his words, that uncharacteristic

blush, something—she was suddenly filled with re-newed optimism.

"It's actually not so hard, if you listen to your heart," she suggested quietly.

To her astonishment, Slade tucked a finger under her chin and tilted her head up, then met her lips with his own. Oblivious to the fascinated onlookers, he kissed her silly. When they were both gasping for breath, he eased away.

"Thanks to you, darlin', I just discovered I have one."

Chapter Fourteen

The prospect of being officially courted made Val's palms sweat. It looked as if all her efforts were finally paying off. Rather than filling her with triumph, the outcome panicked her.

What if she'd been wrong? What if she and Slade weren't suited at all? What if she'd simply been lured by the fact that he was so stubbornly unobtainable? What if it had only been about lust, rather than love? The chase, rather than forever?

After all, what did she really know about love? She'd witnessed the enduring passion between Laurie and Harlan Patrick. She'd seen the quieter love shining in Janet's eyes whenever she spotted Harlan across a room. But in Val's own family, there had been no such example. After her father's death, her mother had never remarried, never even dated very much. Even so, Val had never sensed that it was because her grand passion had died.

No matter how hard she tried, Val couldn't seem to quiet her doubts. What if, what if, what if...? The unanswerable questions tumbled through her head like errant ping-pong balls.

As usual, she'd jumped in feet first, tackling the project of getting Slade's attention as systematically as she would the logistics for one of Laurie's tours. Now it was time to put up or shut up, time to pay the piper, time to fish or cut bait. The clichés tripped through her brain at a dizzying clip.

She needed time for her emotions to switch directions, time to quiet all the nagging fears. She didn't need a man on her doorstep with a handpicked bouquet of flowers and passion in his eyes. That was serious stuff. She'd just been playing a game, or so she'd tried to convince herself during the endless weeks of rejection. Hadn't Laurie pegged that very thing? Hadn't she been the one to suggest that Val had decided Slade wasn't worth her time or effort?

Of course, if that were the case, she should have told him to take his flowers and stuff them, rather than stand there with her heart racing and a smile tugging at her lips. She should have refused to sit on the porch swing, thigh-to-thigh, her hand tucked in his, while he talked nonstop for the first time since she'd known him.

Thinking back on it, she sighed. It had felt so right being there with him. A curious kind of peace had stolen through her, even as her pulse had skipped to an erotic, when-will-he-kiss-me beat. She hadn't thought there could be so much anticipation between a man and a woman who'd already made love, who'd already discovered the most intimate secrets of each other's bodies. But it had been as if they were starting over fresh, as if they'd met for the first time that night, as if there were a million sensual fantasies still to explore.

And she'd agreed to see him again tonight, this time for a real date, just the two of them. They were going to Garden City for dinner and a movie, assuming they could agree on one, given his fondness for action and hers for comedy. She'd had every piece of clothing she'd brought to Texas spread out on her bed at one time or another since dawn, trying to choose the perfect first-date outfit. Half had made their way back into the closet, deemed unsuitable. Unsatisfied with the choices left, she was now reconsidering.

"Did I miss the tornado that blew through here?" Laurie asked, standing in the doorway, her expression quizzical.

"I'm trying to decide what to wear," Val said, considering a simple silk blouse and raw silk slacks in a matching shade of teal. Too plain, she concluded, and tossed them atop the rest for the second time.

"Would I be nuts to point out that you're already dressed?" Laurie inquired, coming in to perch on a chair well out of the path of clothes flying from closet to bed with barely a hesitation in between.

"For tonight," Val replied succinctly, holding up a favorite dress in seduce-me red. "What do you think of this? Too much?"

"Are we talking Slade?"

Val nodded.

"You'll have him cross-eyed and panting."

"Perfect," Val said, hanging the dress on a hook on the closet door so she could stand back and get the full effect. This dress had served her well in the past when she'd wanted to walk into a room and turn up the heat. That was precisely why she'd dismissed it earlier. She wasn't sure heat was what tonight called for. In fact, she was pretty sure it called for caution and quiet reason. If Slade touched her, though, reason was likely to fly straight out the window. She'd missed those insidious caresses that could carry her to a whole other universe.

"Where are you going?" Laurie asked.

"Dinner and the movies."

Laurie shook her head. "Not in that dress. That dress belongs on a dance floor, where he can see it. If you're in a movie, you could be wearing jeans and a T-shirt and it wouldn't matter."

"Good point. We'll go dancing," she said, all but sold on the dress and hang the nagging voice in her head that called for something more sensible. Being in Slade's arms on a dance floor held too much appeal. Being in Slade's arms at all was practically irresistible.

"Wait a second." Laurie was shaking her head before Val finished the statement. "His leg, remember? He might hate the idea of dancing."

"We've danced at parties here," Val argued.

"Among friends."

"He was a little awkward at first, but after that he

was into it,'' Val insisted. She grinned. "Besides, I'm pretty sure he'll be glad to get his hands on me any way he can. He seems to have crossed the great divide between being pursued and becoming the pursuer.''

"And how do you feel being on the other side?" Laurie asked.

She considered the question thoughtfully. "Scared. Giddy. Confused.''

"Confused? Because you're not sure of your feelings for him, after all?''

"That, too. More important, though, I have no idea what turned him around.'' She sank down on the edge of the bed, clutching the heels that matched the red dress. Because it was Laurie asking, she forced herself to dig deep and try to explain her greatest fear. "A week ago, it was all about Annie. Now it seems to be about Slade and me. Did he just wake up one morning and decide he wanted me? Or is this some last-ditch effort to get me for Annie, after all?''

"So you still don't trust his motives?" Laurie asked.

"Would you?"

"Probably not, which is why dating is good. If this is all pretense just to win you over, you'll know soon enough. There's not a man on earth who can actually fake being in love. They just aren't clever enough to fool a woman, not for long, anyway.''

"Are you so sure about that?" Val asked, unable to keep a plaintive note out of her voice. "What if I get suckered in, just the way he wants me to, and find out I'm wrong?''

To her dismay, Laurie actually laughed at the question. "Sweetie, the person hasn't been born yct who can fool you for long. You're very intuitive about human nature. You're warm and generous and caring, which is why Slade wants you in Annie's life and his. He might be able to keep up a pretense for an evening or two, but you'll see through it in a heartbeat. Besides, I don't think Slade's capable of long-term deception. Deep down, he's too honest. That's why he put his cards on the table in the first place. If he's playing a different hand now, it's because he wants to."

"I suppose."

Laurie gestured toward the red dress. "I say go for it. Make the man pay for holding out for so long, for making you doubt what you feel for him."

Val grinned. "That dress is meant to make a grown man weep, isn't it?"

"I imagine that depends on whether or not you decide to let him get you out of it," Laurie replied with a wink. "Don't let Harlan Patrick get a glimpse of it. He'll be down at the barn warning Slade that you're in a take-no-prisoners mood. It will ruin the element of surprise."

Slade took one look at Val and almost abandoned his plans to take her to Garden City. The only place he wanted to take her was bed.

He was pretty sure he'd never seen a dress that slithered over a body as cleverly or as seductively as the red silk scrap she was wearing. Worn in winter, it would guarantee frostbite. It bared shoulders and cleavage and legs. In fact, he was hardpressed to decide what it did cover beyond the necessities. He swallowed hard and tried to find his voice.

"That's...you look..."

She twirled around. "You like it?"

He ran a finger under his collar and wished he weren't wearing a jacket. The temperature had to have gone up a good thirty degrees just since she'd opened the door.

"It's, um... Are you sure you want to wear that just to go to the movies?"

"I thought maybe we'd go dancing instead," she said, striding past him with that provocative sway that was devastating enough when she wasn't encased in red silk. Practically overnight she'd turned into the perfect spokeswoman for sin.

For once, at the mention of dancing, his bum leg was the last thing on his mind. His frantic gaze scanned her back, trying to find one single spot where he could put his hand on it in public without risking heart failure. Couldn't be done, he concluded.

Maybe he could talk her out of dancing between soup and dessert, he decided, following her to the car. He held open the door and practically choked as that fancy slip of a dress slid up her thighs as she got in. He caught the quirk of her lips and realized then and there that she knew exactly the effect she was having. Most parts of his body were already hard, but that smug little smile stiffened his resolve.

Let the woman do her worst. He wasn't going to back down or start running scared. In fact, this evening could get downright fascinating if he decided to call her on her game. Unless he counted the one and only time hc'd taken Val into his bed, it had been a long time since he'd let a little casual flirting turn serious.

"Dancing it is," he said, as he slid behind the wheel and gave her a slow, thorough once-over that could have melted steel. He almost chuckled at the alarm that flickered in her eyes, right before she blinked and looked away.

He'd been planning dinner in a casual restaurant that was popular with some of the ranch hands, followed by a movie. He'd counted on being able to slip an arm around her shoulders or maybe snuggle her hand in his own while they'd sat in the darkened theater. That dress and her desire to go dancing had thrown his plans into disarray. He wasn't sure he knew of any place in Garden City that could withstand the shock value of that dress. He glanced over at her.

"Did you have someplace special in mind? I'm afraid my visits to Garden City haven't taken me to the kind of place that dress belongs," he admitted.

Amusement flashed in her eyes again. "And what kind of place do you think it belongs?" she inquired in a tone that challenged him to tred diplomatically.

"Someplace fancy. Elegant. You know, where they do the waltz, instead of the two-step." He didn't say he was afraid anything as energetic as the two-step would have her shimmying right out of that dress.

She grinned. "Good answer. Laurie mentioned that the Garden City Hotel has a new dining room that brings in a band on Saturdays."

It would also have beds upstairs. How convenient,

Slade thought, already well beyond the last dance in his imagination. Truth be told, he wasn't sure he could hold out past the appetizers.

"Sounds good," he said, his throat tight.

Those were the last words he managed to choke out until they reached the neighboring town and its quaint historic district. The Garden City Hotel was a very old, wooden structure that maintained its image as one of the city's original buildings. It would have suited the set of a Western movie just fine.

Inside, however, was another story. The owners had updated and refurbished the interior to create an elegant ambiance. Slade figured the restaurant was guaranteed to blow his food budget for the month. Val was worth it, though. She was the kind of woman who belonged in a place like this. In fact, she'd probably grown accustomed to luxuries while she was on the road with Laurie. He wondered if she could accept that luxuries like this came along once in a blue moon on a ranch hand's salary.

Heads turned as she sashayed across the lobby to the dining room. Slade credited the dress for the reaction, but the truth was Val in burlap could have made heads turn. She had a kind of presence that no other woman he'd dated had had. The Adams women had it. He'd always figured it came with money, but maybe it had more to do with self-confidence. Val exuded it. A pride and possessiveness he had no right to feel welled up inside him just the same.

The dining room was lit with candles on every table, setting a romantic mood—or trying to keep folks from seeing the prices on the menu, Slade thought cynically. A small band was tuning up on a raised platform at the far end of the room. The dance floor in front of them was large enough to accommodate a dozen couples and no more. The whole ambiance was intimate, suggesting that those lucky enough to be there were part of a very exclusive club.

The maître d' clucked over their lack of a reservation until Slade slipped him a twenty-dollar bill. Amazingly enough a table right beside the dance floor suddenly became available. Val followed the man in his stiff black suit, while Slade brought up the rear and admired the view. He figured if his heart gave out before the night was over, he'd die a happy man.

"*Madame,*" the maître d' said, holding Val's chair. He kept his gaze discreetly averted as she sat down, Slade noticed. Good thing, he thought. He would have hated to have to punch the guy out for ogling her legs.

"Nice place," he said, after they were alone.

Her eyes twinkled merrily. "Do you really like it?"

"What's not to like? The music's promising. The menu weighs a ton and the wine list has enough French on it to guarantee there's a decent champagne on there."

"Champagne?"

"It's not just for celebrations, darlin'. And even if it were, I'd say this occasion calls for it."

"Oh, really? Why is that?"

"It's our first date." He glanced over the wine list, beckoned the wine steward and ordered a bottle of Dom Pérignon.

Val's eyes widened with surprise. "Isn't that a little expensive? A nice, domestic white wine would do."

"Not tonight," he said tersely, determined to prove he knew how to treat a lady. There'd been a time when he'd swilled down fancy champagne after every rodeo victory. Despite his preference for an occasional beer and a burger, he knew his way around in a place like this. For reasons he couldn't entirely explain, he set out to prove it. "Mind if I order for both of us?"

Val gave him a puzzled look, but nodded.

He ordered escargots, chateaubriand for two, and salads after the meal. "We'll decide on dessert later," he told the waiter.

One glance across the table told him he'd startled her with his choices, with his easy familiarity with the menu.

"Snails?" she whispered in a choked voice.

"Sure. The place is French, isn't it? They're a delicacy."

"If you say so."

He grinned at her reaction, then leaned across the table to confide, "Personally, I stick to dipping the bread in all that garlic butter, but you can do what you want."

Laughter bubbled up and erupted. "Oh, thank God. I was terrified you were actually going to expect me to eat them."

"Nope. We'll just admire them for a while, then send them on their way."

"Won't the waiter wonder about that?"

"Not in a place like this," Slade decreed. "They're paid to keep their thoughts to themselves."

After the champagne had been poured, he held out his hand. "Care to dance?"

Val stood up at once and moved gracefully into his arms. The band had started with something slow and old-fashioned, a Glenn Miller tune, if Slade wasn't mistaken. The tempo made it easy for him to keep time. Holding Val inspired him.

He could hardly tell where soft skin gave way to silky fabric beneath his touch. Her scent rose to fill his head with thoughts of being outdoors in a garden, with her in his arms under the stars. The brush of her thighs against his made his pulse pound and sent blood rushing to a part of his anatomy that had been on the verge of arousal ever since he'd caught his first glimpse of her earlier. Val knew it, too, but instead of pulling away, she tucked herself even closer, snuggling against him in a way that was downright dangerous.

"You're playing with fire, sweetheart," he warned softly.

Wide eyes gazed up at him. "Is that so?"

"Another couple of minutes and we'll miss dinner altogether."

A smile came and went. "It's just snails and steak. We can have that anytime."

Slade gave her a startled look. She'd sounded half-serious. "What are you suggesting? Since you were the one who wanted to go dancing and this is our very first turn around the floor, I think you'd better spell it out for me."

She gave him a brazen look that went with the red dress. "I'm suggesting we grab that bottle of champagne and make a run for it. I hear the rooms have really, really big beds."

Slade's pulse ricocheted wildly. "And if they're all taken?"

"Use your imagination, cowboy. It's been working overtime all night, anyway."

But nothing he'd imagined had involved making love in the front seat of a truck. "You stay put and fend off those snails. I'll get a room," he declared with grim determination.

Ten minutes later, they were upstairs in a room dominated by a king-size bed. The heat that had been simmering on low between them all night turned into a bonfire when he discovered that all Val had on under that dress were panties and a red garter belt. He swallowed hard as she stood before him and daintily rolled down her hose to remove them.

"Lady, you are dangerous," he murmured as he touched a fingertip to one nipple and watched it harden. When he touched the same place with his tongue, she gasped and all but came apart.

"Now," she pleaded. "Please, Slade. I want you inside me now."

Her cry was almost his undoing. He slipped inside her moist heat with all the best intentions to take it slow, but she wouldn't allow it. The frantic rise and fall of her hips demanded a pace that tugged him toward oblivion. When her body shattered with a violent climax, she carried him along, then sank back against the pillows with a sigh of pure contentment.

Still trying to catch his breath, he regarded her with amusement. "Pretty pleased with yourself, aren't you?"

"I have no idea what you mean," she claimed, her expression all innocence despite the position of their bodies.

"This evening has gone exactly the way you planned." It sounded more like an accusation than he'd intended.

Her gaze darkened. "Are you complaining?"

"About this? Never," he said. "I'm just a little confused about how we ended up here."

"We're two adults, Slade. If we want to sleep together, we certainly can. We're not hurting anyone."

"So this is just about sex?" he asked, his tone lethal. "You had some kind of an itch and I happened to be around to scratch it?"

She blinked at the question and something that could have been hurt shadowed her eyes, but she recovered quickly. "That's a little crude, but yes," she said.

Slade rolled to the side of the bed and sat up. He was suddenly so furious it took every ounce of restraint he possessed to keep from yelling at her.

"I think we must have gotten our signals crossed," he said eventually. "You see, when I climbed into this bed, it was with the intention of making love to a woman I care about, just like it was the last time we were together."

"You weren't making love that first night," Val retorted. "You were striking a bargain."

Slade felt as if she'd punched him in the gut.

"That's what this was about? Some sort of payback? A signal, maybe, that you're willing to play the game my way?"

"Exactly." Her chin wobbled, but her eyes flashed fire.

"Well, I'm not," he said dully. "The next time you and I make love, it will be on our wedding night."

"And what if I won't marry you?"

"Then this will have to hold us both till hell freezes over," he said, yanking on his clothes.

When he was dressed, he tossed her red silk dress at her. "I think it's time to go home."

Only then did he dare to look at her. A huge tear was rolling down her cheek.

"Don't do that," he said sharply.

"What?"

"Don't cry. Don't act as if I've hurt your feelings. You were the one who wanted to turn this into something cold and impersonal."

"You're wrong," she whispered. "That's not what I wanted at all."

"What then?"

She sighed heavily and began to get dressed.

Slade grabbed her arm and held her still, then waited until she finally gazed into his eyes. "What did you want?"

"I wanted you to admit how you really felt about me," she said. "I guess I know now, don't I?"

"And what do you think you know?"

"That you want me."

"And?"

"That's it," she insisted.

Slade muttered an expletive under his breath, then dragged her back into his arms. Only after he'd kissed her thoroughly did he step back. "Next time think harder."

Chapter Fifteen

Nothing about the date had gone the way Val envisioned. She'd wanted to tempt Slade, wanted to drive him a little crazy, but she hadn't meant to lure him straight to a hotel room.

Nor had she intended to insinuate that their relationship was about nothing more than sex. She'd insulted him and cheapened herself.

"Why, why, why?" she moaned as she sipped her first cup of coffee the next morning.

"Why what?" Laurie asked, joining her at the kitchen table.

"Why did you let me wear that red dress?"

"*Let* you?" Laurie echoed. "Could I have stopped you?"

Val heaved a sigh. "No. I suppose not," she conceded.

"Did it work?"

"In a manner of speaking. He couldn't wait to get me out of it."

"And your problem with that is?"

Before Val could answer, Laurie glanced up and immediately got to her feet. "Don't mind me," she said with obviously forced cheer. "I think I'll take my decaf into the music room. Lots to do. See you."

Listening to the suddenly inane chattering of her friend, Val followed the direction of Laurie's gaze and found Slade standing on the doorstep, shifting uncomfortably from foot to foot. She should have guessed, should have been prepared for what the sight of him would do to her. She wanted him every bit as badly now as she had the night before when she'd let her hormones drive reason from her mind.

"Mind if I come in?" he asked, when Laurie had gone.

Val shrugged, feigning an indifference she was far from feeling. "Suit yourself."

Rotating his hat in his hands, he sat down across from her and peered at her earnestly. "Look, I don't know exactly what happened last night."

"Oh, really?"

He scowled at her, then at the hat, finally tossing it aside as if it were a distraction. "You know what I mean. It was like we took a giant leap from the first date to the fifth with no stops in between. I want you to know that wasn't what I had in mind when I asked you out."

"What did you have in mind?" she asked, curious

about what might have happened if that red dress had stayed in the closet.

"Starting over, just you and me, trying to find out if what we're feeling is just plain crazy or something real."

As if the explanation made him uncomfortable, he got back to his feet and busied himself pouring a cup of coffee before rejoining her.

"Look, you know I made a lot of mistakes with Annie's mom," he began again, that earnest look back in his eyes. "I never intended to get caught up in something like that again. And you and me, well, there are a lot of strikes against us. We're not exactly from the same world."

He was so serious, so determined to set things right, that she couldn't help leaning forward to confide, "I've gotta tell you, if your world contains escargots, we really don't have a lot to talk about."

A half smile came and went at her teasing. "I was trying to impress you, prove I could be the kind of man you're used to. It's not my fault you wore a dress that could make a man forget his own name, much less his intentions."

Val sighed. "That dress was probably a mistake. It was supposed to get your attention, but it was definitely a fifth-date dress."

"I've been doing a lot of thinking since last night. I'd like to try this again," Slade said, studying her worriedly. "Unless you figure we don't stand a chance."

"I've never thought that."

"Good." He rose, grabbed his hat from the chair

where it had landed, shoved it onto his head and moved toward the door. He had it open and one foot out, when he turned back. "By the way, have your reached your own conclusions about what happened in that room last night?"

Val held back a grin. "I'm still thinking about it. Could be you'll have to refresh my memory."

He laughed at the taunt. "Fifth date, darlin', and not a minute before."

Val figured they'd better cram dates two, three and four into a very tight timetable, beginning with a picnic by the creek tonight. Just to be sure they didn't skip ahead, maybe she'd invite Annie along.

Of course, that would defeat the purpose of the two of them spending time alone to discover just how suited they might be. She was still debating with herself when Annie inadvertently solved the problem by announcing she was going to watch a swimming and diving meet with her diving instructor and some of the other students.

"We won't be back till real late," she told Val pointedly. "In case you and Daddy want to go somewhere."

Val grinned at the lack of subtlety. "Thank you for letting me know."

"You weren't out very late last night," Annie said, her expression troubled. "How come?"

"We decided to have an early evening. Your dad has to get up before dawn."

"But he doesn't need much sleep. You can stay out as late as you want next time," Annie advised her.

"I'm sure your dad will be pleased to know he doesn't have a curfew," Val said. "Now why don't you get your things together and I'll take you into town, so your instructor doesn't have to drive all the way out here?"

"She won't mind. You should probably take a bubble bath or something."

A few minutes later, as she was sitting in a steaming bath filled with fragrant bubbles, Val concluded that she was in serious trouble if she'd started taking courting advice from a kid.

Still, she felt especially feminine in her sundress and sandals as she waited on Slade's porch with a picnic hamper. It was almost dusk when he finally came dragging up the path, looking beat. His expression brightened ever so slightly at the sight of her.

"What are you doing here?"

"We have a second date tonight," she told him, gesturing toward the hamper. "Nothing fancy. Just a picnic by the creek."

He regarded her with a puzzled expression. "Did we make these plans this morning?"

"Not exactly. I just seized the moment," she admitted. "Annie's gone off for the evening. She informed me she won't be home till late. *Real* late."

A grin tugged at his lips. "Is that so?"

"Do you think a shower will revive you or would you rather do this another night?"

"Let me try the shower and see how it goes."

When he returned, his hair was still damp, but he was freshly shaved and smelled of soap. "If you have fried chicken in that basket, you will make me a happy man.''

"With coleslaw and potato salad," she said. "And a couple of cold beers.''

"Ah, perfect. Now I'm ecstatic.'' He held out his hand. "Shall we?''

Gestures like that still surprised her. A few days ago she would have judged it to be totally out of character. Now she sensed that he was literally and figuratively reaching out to her. She hesitated, then tucked her hand in his.

It was cooler down by the creek. Val spread out the blanket she'd brought, then took out their supper. Slade leaned back against the trunk of a tree and accepted a plate. They ate in silence, but Val concluded it was the kind of companionable silence that fell between friends. Used to nonstop conversation, she realized that the quiet had its own rewards, especially when Slade's gaze caught hers and held until her breath clogged in her throat.

There was a dusting of stars across the sky by the time they'd finished eating. A sliver of moon hung in the velvety darkness. Slade stretched out on the blanket and sighed with contentment.

"Never thought much of picnics before now," he said.

"Why?''

"Seemed like a lot of trouble to go to, when you could eat the same food sitting at the kitchen table.''

"Has tonight changed your mind?''

"Just about.'' He gave her a lazy once-over. "I have a hunch if you were to stretch out here beside me and tuck your head on my shoulder, I'd reach a whole different conclusion.''

Val leaned down to stare into his eyes. ''Second date, remember?''

''Got it,'' he said, laughter in his eyes. ''But don't be surprised if I try to steal a third-date kind of kiss.''

She sighed as she settled against him. ''I think I'd be disappointed if you didn't.''

She felt the soft brush of his lips against her forehead and closed her eyes. Desire spiraled through her, but so did that same sense of peace she'd felt a few nights ago. She was beginning to see that her instincts all those months ago had been right. Slade really was the right man for her.

Val was making him jump through hoops, but Slade supposed he deserved it. First he'd tried to get her to marry him just so Annie would have a mom again. Then he'd dragged her up to a hotel room on their first real date. He hadn't even let her start her dinner, much less finish it. Not that she'd complained. In fact, she'd been as eager as he'd been, but it had been the wrong way to go about getting reacquainted. Now he'd established some weird dating timetable that required him to keep his hands off of her for two more dates.

He supposed they'd go by quickly enough. Val seemed almost as anxious as he was to get them behind her. In the past few days she'd dreamed up a million things she'd always wanted to do, dropping hints the way a bee buzzed around spreading pollen. Then she waited to see if he picked up on them.

She wanted to go dancing again, despite the way the last time had turned out.

"I haven't really gotten the hang of the two-step yet," she said, making it clear that she had an entirely different sort of evening in mind. She didn't seem to care that he had a bum leg, that he was as clumsy as a man could be and still stay on two feet. But he did it, just to get the third date out of the way, or so he told himself. The truth was he had a good time once he got the hang of holding her in his arms and swaying to the music, instead of trying to move around the dance floor. She didn't seem to mind so much that she still didn't know the two-step by the end of the evening.

When Val wasn't dreaming up tortures for him, she was planning little outings for all three of them. There were more picnics, mostly with Annie along, which meant they weren't considered part of their dating schedule. That could have been irksome, but it wasn't once he got the hang of sneaking a kiss whenever Annie wasn't looking. They went to diving meets with Annie and her friends. They took in several movies and ate enough pizza to qualify as honorary Italians.

One night as they finished their meal, several of Annie's friends came into the restaurant. She ran off to talk to them. Slade watched her laughing and felt something deep inside him shift.

"She seems happy," he said cautiously, not quite ready to believe his eyes.

Val regarded him with surprise. "Of course she's happy. Why wouldn't she be?"

"She wasn't when she came to live with me."

"She was scared, Slade. She'd felt abandoned. She didn't believe you wanted her here with you. That's all changed the past couple of months. You're a good father."

He dismissed the praise. "What kind of father abandons his kid in the first place?"

"The kind who's going through a tough time. It's not as if you left her with strangers. She was with her grandparents. They gave her plenty of love and attention."

"But it wasn't the same," he insisted, echoing what Annie had told him on more than one occasion.

"Not the same, but the best you could do for her at the time. Someday she'll understand that. She's already forgiven you. Isn't it time you forgave yourself?"

He was stunned by her words. "Is that what you think I've been doing? Blaming myself? Paying penance?"

Val nodded. "That's certainly the way it looks from here. I even think that's why you asked me to marry you, out of guilt over having failed Annie once before. You decided to give her the one thing you thought she really needed—a mom."

He supposed there was more than a little truth in that. "No wonder you turned me down."

"It was the gesture of a loving father, albeit a misguided one. All Annie really needed was to have her dad back in her life. Look how she's blossomed."

"You're as responsible for that as I am," he insisted.

She grinned. "Okay, we'll share the credit."

He reached for her hand. "You're an incredible woman, Val Harding."

Color flared in her cheeks at the compliment. "Thank you," she whispered in a choked voice.

"Don't you dare cry," he commanded, alarmed by her reaction. "I'll never be able to say anything nice again, if all it does is make you weepy."

"Weepy's not a bad thing."

"Maybe from where you're sitting," he grumbled. "It makes me crazy. I keep thinking I've gone and ruined things again."

"Hasn't anyone ever explained the difference between happy tears and sad ones?"

"Doesn't matter. They all make me crazy," he repeated. "Suzanne used to turn on the waterworks at the drop of a hat, because she knew she'd get her way."

"Manipulative tears are a whole other ball game," Val said. "It's not a technique I'm fond of."

He studied her intently, then nodded. "No, I don't imagine you've ever had to resort to tears to get what you wanted. You're probably the most direct woman I've ever known."

"Is that good or bad?"

He shrugged. "I haven't decided yet. I always know where I stand, that's for sure."

"And you always will," she assured him. "I can't hide what I'm feeling, Slade. I won't do it, even for you, even if it makes you uncomfortable. That's why I didn't even try to hide my interest in you from the day we met."

Slade thought maybe just this once he could use that disconcerting directness of hers to his advantage, maybe get a reading on just what she was thinking about the two of them these days. He was running out of courting ideas. They'd long since skipped past the fifth date, even if he hadn't tried to get her into his bed again. He was just about ready to pop the big marriage question again, but he didn't want to risk another rejection.

"So," he said, casually. "How do you think this dating thing is going?"

Amusement spread across her face. "Just fine from my perspective. How about yours?"

"Can I be honest?"

"Of course."

"To tell you the truth, it's getting on my nerves."

She went absolutely still. "Oh?"

He recognized that deadly tone with its undercurrent of hurt. "I want more, Val. I'm not a kid. I'm way past dating."

"Maybe I'm not understanding you. What is it you want?"

"I want to take it to the next level."

Her gaze narrowed. "Which is?"

He was about to say marriage, but at the last second his courage failed him. "A relationship," he declared. "I want us to have a relationship."

To his astonishment, she began to laugh.

"What?" he demanded indignantly.

"Oh, Slade, you wonderful, sweet man."

"What?" he repeated.

"What exactly do you think we've been having all these weeks?"

He struggled to find a word, but got lost somewhere between friendship and sex. He figured neither description would earn him any points.

"A relationship?" he suggested cautiously.

"Exactly," she said.

Well, damn, he was better at it than he'd thought. And it wasn't nearly as terrifying as he'd imagined it would be. Maybe he was ready to take that leap to the next level—the highest level—after all.

Just not tonight.

Chapter Sixteen

Val had been all but certain that Slade was going to propose the night before. An Italian restaurant wasn't the place she would have chosen for such a momentous occasion, nor would she have had Annie nearby. But that hadn't mattered when she'd seen the glint in his eye and heard him fumbling for words. She'd been sure she knew what was coming.

Her heart had climbed into her throat. Her palms had begun to sweat. She'd looked into his eyes and seen what she thought was love shining there. Hope had blossomed deep inside her.

Then he'd blurted out that he wanted them to have a relationship. What kind of a suggestion was that? She hadn't been able to hold back the laugh, even though she'd seen right away that she'd hurt him.

How on earth was she supposed to get *him* to the next level? At this rate, they'd both be confined to rocking chairs on the front porch by the time he got around to asking her to marry him.

"Do you think I should propose to Slade?" she asked idly, while Laurie was rehearsing the last new song for her album.

Laurie's nimble fingers strummed a discordant screech on the guitar. "Excuse me?"

"It wasn't a trick question. Do you think I should propose to Slade?"

"Not in a million years," Laurie said adamantly.

"Why not?"

"For starters, it's the one thing in life that is mostly the man's prerogative."

"Even a man who can't make up his mind?"

"Especially a man who can't make up his mind. Give him time, Val. He'll come around to the idea all on his own. If he doesn't, then it wasn't meant to be. I don't think it's smart to try to shove him off this particular cliff before he's ready."

"What if he's just too scared to spit the words out?"

"Do you think that's Slade's problem?"

"Honestly, yes. I could have sworn he was going to do it last night, but at the last second he shifted gears and said he wanted us to have a relationship."

"That's progress."

"No, it's not," Val said impatiently. "That's what we've been doing all along, having a relationship."

"Perhaps he meant an *intimate* relationship."

Val considered that. "Could be." She winced as she thought of the way the light had died in his eyes at her laughter. "I probably shouldn't have laughed."

Laurie groaned. "You didn't."

"Afraid so."

"That'll do a lot to build up his courage."

"Which brings me back to why I think I should do the proposing. It'll take the pressure off."

Laurie stared at her intently. "You're going to do it no matter what I say, aren't you?"

Val reached a decision and nodded. "Yes. I think I am."

"When?"

"Tonight," she said. "I think I'll take him flowers. Or do you think I should take him a plate of fried chicken? He really likes that."

Laurie sighed. "Just don't take your own engagement ring."

Val regarded her indignantly. "I would never do that. Some things the man has to do."

"I'm relieved you can see that," Laurie said wryly. "Let me know how it turns out."

To Val's chagrin, Laurie didn't exactly sound as if she expected a happy ending.

Slade considered the disaster in the restaurant the night before and wondered how to avoid a repeat. He was tired of this crazy limbo they were in, but for the life of him he couldn't see a way to end it. He wasn't the kind of man who knew how to string pretty words together. Just look at the way he'd blurted out that nonsense about wanting a relationship. No wonder she had laughed. He would have been better off if he'd just shown her the engagement ring he'd bought, and hoped she'd get the message.

He was pretty sure that Val still didn't believe that this was just between the two of them, that he loved her. He wasn't sure he had the words to tell her all that was in his heart. He stood in front of the mirror over the mantel and tried to find some eloquent way of expressing it. Once he'd said her name, he choked.

"Daddy, what are you doing?" Annie said, coming into the room to peer up at him quizzically. "I heard you talking to yourself."

His cheeks turned brick red. "Nothing."

"You said Val's name. I heard it." Her expression filled with sudden understanding. "You're rehearsing, aren't you?"

"Rehearsing what?"

"A proposal," she said excitedly. "You're finally going to ask her to marry you. I found the ring in your pocket and I've been waiting and waiting. What's taking so long?"

"There's a lot to think about."

"Well, just do it. It can't be that hard."

"That's easy for you to say. I tried it last night and blew it."

Annie's eyes widened. "You did? What did you say?"

"Never mind. Let's just say that I didn't get it right."

"Okay, here's what we'll do," she said decisively. "I'll tell you what to say."

"I don't think so."

"Why not? You've got to get it right this time, Daddy. It could be our last chance."

She ran off for a piece of paper and a pencil. Then she laid out a romantic spiel that even he had to admit was better than anything he'd come up with. When he'd finished reading it to himself, she gestured for him to get down on one knee.

"You say it," she said, in the imperious manner of a director determined to coach great theater out of an amateur.

"I feel ridiculous," he told his daughter. "I cannot get down on one knee and say this stuff, especially not to my own daughter."

"I'm not Annie now. I'm Val. Besides, you want her to say yes, don't you?" the ten-year-old matchmaker asked. "Just pretend you're gazing real deep into Val's eyes and say it."

Slade felt like an idiot. He drew in a deep breath and forced himself to read from the paper Annie had given him. "Val, I know I don't have much of a way with words, but you mean the world to me. I never thought I'd fall in love again, but you made it easy. You opened your heart and let me in."

"Us," Annie corrected. "She let us in." She pointed to the page. "See, that's what I wrote."

"This is my proposal, squirt. You can make your own, if you think mine's not good enough."

Annie rolled her eyes. "Daddy, kids don't ask people to marry them. Say it again."

This time Slade managed to get most of the words out without faltering before he realized that the intended bride was actually standing in the doorway, openmouthed and holding a bouquet of flowers in one hand and a foil-covered plate of what smelled like fried chicken in the other. He awkwardly got to his feet, cursing his gimpy leg.

"Guess I stole my own thunder, didn't I?" he asked, gazing into her eyes, which were shimmering with tears. He wished to hell he were better at reading the distinction between happy tears and sad ones. If he lived to be a hundred, he didn't think he'd get it.

The plate wobbled and he grabbed for it. Once it was safely on the table, he said, "I've got a ring around here somewhere, if you'd like me to try it again."

Annie ran off. When she came back, she slipped the ring into his hand, then vanished, though he suspected she hadn't gone out of earshot.

"What you said before—did you mean it?" Val asked.

"That I love you? Yes, Val, I do love you," he said softly. "Annie may have done the coaching, but the sentiments are all mine. I'm sorry it took me so long to recognize the feelings for what they were. I'm sorrier still that it took me so long to tell you."

Her gaze, brimming with more tears, searched his face. "You're sure about that? You're absolutely sure you love me, that you're not being forced into saying this by your daughter?''

"I've never been more sure of anything in my life. Will you marry me?"

"Us," Annie hissed from just outside.

Val chuckled at the intrusion. "Anybody who'd take the two of you on must like living dangerously."

"I have it on the best authority that you do," he pointed out. "Why else would a born-and-bred city slicker turn in her heels for a pair of boots?"

A smile spread slowly across her face and he knew then that it was going to be all right.

"Yes," she said, moving into his arms. "Yes, I will marry you."

As her arms came around his neck, the bouquet fell to the floor, strewing it with rose petals.

After he'd kissed her thoroughly and slipped the ring on her finger, he stood back and studied her face. "So what was with the flowers and the food?"

She blushed furiously. "Oh, just a little peace offering."

Slade didn't believe it for a minute. "Val?"

"I think it's better if we just leave it at that," she insisted, kissing him in a blatant effort to distract him.

It might have worked, too, if it hadn't been for that guilty gleam in her eyes. Suddenly he knew. "You were going to propose, weren't you?"

"Never," she said, as if shocked by the idea.

"You were."

"I was not."

"I would have said yes," he teased. "But you already knew that, didn't you?"

"Okay, I was hoping," she admitted finally. She touched a finger to his lips. "But I'm so glad you said the words first. I'd have hated telling our grandchildren that I had to talk their granddaddy into marrying me."

"What grandchildren?" Annie demanded, coming out from hiding. "All you've got is me."

"Believe me," Slade said, ruffling her hair, "you are the best start to our family we could possibly have."

"Start?" Val mouthed.

"I figure a couple more wouldn't hurt. Now that I'm getting the hang of this fatherhood thing, I'd like to put it to use."

"No boys," Annie insisted. "I want sisters."

"I'm not sure you'll have any say in the matter," Slade informed her. "Mother Nature has her own way of deciding what's right."

"Well, if I can't pick sisters, can I at least pick when the wedding's going to be?"

Val grinned at her enthusiasm. "What did you have in mind?"

"Christmas," she said at once.

"Why Christmas?" Slade asked.

"Because it's still a long ways away and you can't get married till my hair grows out. I ain't looking like a boy in all the pictures."

Slade and Val exchanged a glance.

"I think a Christmas wedding sounds just about perfect," Val said, eyes shining.

"It's one way to guarantee I won't forget our anniversary." Slade teased.

"Oh, Daddy," Annie moaned. "That's not romantic."

"No," Val agreed. "Your father could use a little help in that regard." She winked at him. "But we're working on it."

Slade Sutton and Val Harding had a Christmas wedding that was perfect down to the last detail. Val saw to it with her usual brisk efficiency. Or would have if she hadn't been such a nervous wreck. A very pregnant Laurie picked up the slack and saw to it that nothing was overlooked.

The church was the same one where generations of Adamses had been married. Already decorated for the season, it was filled with white poinsettias and lit by candles for the evening ceremony.

The bride wore white satin and very high heels, even though no one could see just what they did for her legs. She knew from experience that Slade's imagination was vivid enough to get the picture. She figured one glimpse of those heels and he'd haul her off on their honeymoon even before they cut the cake.

The groom wore a Western-cut tuxedo.

The maid of honor was resplendent in a green velvet gown she insisted made her look like a very ripe watermelon. The best man thought otherwise. He thought she was the most beautiful pregnant woman he had ever seen.

And the bridesmaid—to everyone's astonishment—wore a red velvet dress trimmed in satin, and had her hair fixed up in curls. To her amazement everyone said she was the prettiest girl in the church.

She knew better, though. Annie knew the prettiest woman there was her new mom.

*   *   *   *   *

Watch for Hardy Jones's story—
and when this sworn-to-be-single cowboy falls,
he falls hard—coming in January 2000,
from Silhouette Special Edition.
It's Sherryl Woods's next installment of

AND BABY MAKES THREE.
THE NEXT GENERATION—

THE COWBOY AND THE NEW YEAR'S BABY

And now,
turn the page
for a sneak preview of

AFTER TEX,

the exciting new novel by

Sherryl Woods,

coming in October 1999,
from MIRA Books

By the time they turned into the long, winding drive to the ranch, the sun had vanished behind a bank of heavy, gray clouds. Snow, thick and wet, splashed against the windshield. The air, when Megan finally stepped out of the car's warmth, was raw.

Leaving the luggage to Jake, she ran toward the front door, only to skid to a halt on the porch when the door was opened by a child or eight or nine, her eyes puffy and red from crying, her hair a tangle of thick auburn curls.

"Who're you?" she demanded, glaring up at Megan.

"I'm Megan O'Rourke," Megan responded automatically, then realized that she was the one who ought to be asking questions. "Who are you?"

"I'm Tess. I live here," she declared with a hint of defiance.

Megan stared at her, as shocked as if she'd uttered an especially vile obscenity. "That can't be," she murmured, just as Jake bounded onto the porch and tucked a supporting hand under her elbow to guide her inside.

The child regarded him with only slightly less hostility. "We're about to have dinner. You gonna stay again?"

Jake ignored the lack of warmth in the invitation and grinned. "Chicken and dumplings?"

She nodded. "Mrs. Gomez said they were her favorites," she said, gesturing toward Megan. She gave Megan another defiant look. "I hate chicken and dumplings."

That said, she stomped off in the direction of the kitchen. Megan watched her go, then sank down on the nearest chair. "Who is that child and what is she doing here?" she demanded, already dreading the answer. There wasn't a doubt in her mind that whatever Jake's response was, she was going to hate it. That red hair all but shouted that the girl was an O'Rourke.

"Her name is Tess," Jake began.

"She told me that much."

"Tess O'Rourke."

The confirmation sent a shudder washing over her. Her gaze shot to his. "Please don't tell me..." Megan couldn't even say it.

"She's your grandfather's daughter," he said. "Which technically makes her your aunt, but I think you can be forgiven if you decide not to call her Auntie Tess."

She had hoped for a distant cousin, maybe. Even a sister, but an *aunt?* It was ludicrous. "I don't believe this," she murmured. "I don't believe it."

"Believe it."

"But how?"

"The usual way, I imagine. All I know for sure is that Tex had just found out about her himself a few months back. She was abandoned on his doorstep. He didn't think he should mention it on the phone.''

"Yeah, I can see why he might not want to," Megan said wryly.

Jake was studying her sympathetically. "You okay?"

"Just peachy."

"Good, because it gets more interesting."

Megan shook her head. "I don't think I can handle anything more interesting."

"You'll adapt. Isn't that what you do best?"

He said it in a way that sounded more accusatory than complimentary. She didn't have time to analyze why before he went on.

"According to your grandfather's will, you are officially Tess's legal guardian."

"No," she whispered, stunned not only by the concept, but by the weight of the responsibility. She hadn't planned on having kids, at least not without going through the usual preparations—marriage, pregnancy, nine months to get used to the idea. She hadn't even had nine seconds.

Megan tried to imagine taking a kid back to New York with her, fitting her into a life already stretched to its limits. Her imagination, always vivid, failed miserably.

"There has to be another way, Mrs. Gomez..."

"She'll help out, certainly," Jake said. "She's told me she intends to stay on here as long as you need her."

"Well, that's it, then," she said gratefully, relieved to have the issue settled so expeditiously.

"Not quite," Jake said. "You can't just dump Tess with Mrs. Gomez and take off."

"Why the hell can't I?" she all but shouted as panic flooded through her.

"Because Tex has spelled it all out in his will. I'll give you a copy of the letter."

His intimate familiarity with the details of Tex's wishes stirred suspicion. "How do you know so much about Tex's will?" she asked, gaze narrowed.

"Because I'm the one who drew it up. Believe me, it's airtight."

Megan wondered just how many shocks her heart could take before she wound up in a grave right next to Tex. "You're a lawyer?"

"A damned good one, if I do say so myself. You renege on the terms Tex has spelled out and the ranch is up for grabs." His expression turned triumphant. "In other words, it'll be all but mine, Megan, and there won't be a damned thing you can do to stop it."

Silhouette ® SPECIAL EDITION®

LINDSAY McKENNA

**delivers two more exciting books in her
heart-stopping new series:**

MORGAN'S MERCENARIES
III
THE HUNTERS

Coming in July 1999:
HUNTER'S WOMAN
Special Edition #1255
Ty Hunter wanted his woman back from the moment he set his
piercing gaze on her. For despite the protest on Dr. Catt Alborak's
soft lips, Ty was on a mission to give the stubborn beauty
everything he'd foolishly denied her once—his heart,
his soul—and most of all, his child....

And coming in October 1999:
HUNTER'S PRIDE
Special Edition #1274
Devlin Hunter had a way with the ladies, but when it came to his
job as a mercenary, the brooding bachelor worked alone. Until
his latest assignment paired him up with Kulani Dawson, a feisty
beauty whose tender vulnerabilities brought out his every
protective instinct—and chipped away at his proud vow to never
fall in love....

Look for the exciting series finale in early 2000—when
MORGAN'S MERCENARIES: THE HUNTERS comes to
Silhouette Desire®!

Available at your favorite retail outlet.

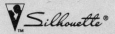

Silhouette ®

If you enjoyed what you just read,
then we've got an offer you can't resist!

Take 2 bestselling love stories FREE!
Plus get a FREE surprise gift!

SILHOUETTE BOOKS
is proud to announce the arrival of

THE BABY OF THE MONTH CLUB:

the latest installment of author
Marie Ferrarella's
popular miniseries.

When pregnant Juliette St. Claire met Gabriel Saldana than she discovered he wasn't the struggling artist he claimed to be. An undercover agent, Gabriel had been sent to Juliette's gallery to nab his prime suspect: Juliette herself. But when he discovered her innocence, would he win back Juliette's heart and convince her that he was the daddy her baby needed?

Don't miss Juliette's induction into
THE BABY OF THE MONTH CLUB
in September 1999.
Available at your favorite retail outlet.

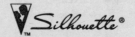